*Powerful, prominent, proud—the Oklahoma Wentworths'
greatest fortune was family. So when they discovered that
pregnant mom-to-be Sabrina Jensen was carrying the
newest Wentworth heir—and had vanished without a
trace—they vowed to...Follow That Baby!*

Sabrina Jensen: After her
daughter's delivery, the diner
waitress turned doting mom finally
stopped running, taking up residence
at the Wentworth estate...where she
received the *second* shock of her life
when she discovered her baby's
daddy *wasn't* dead.

Jack Wentworth: An undercover mission gone awry
had separated the lovestruck CEO from the woman
of his dreams. But before he could stake his claim on
mother and child, he needed to confront his
ultimate betrayer....

Trey McGill: Jack's turncoat friend was now his
family's greatest enemy. Only the strong would
survive the final showdown....

* * * *

Don't miss this exciting conclusion to Follow That Baby!

Dear Reader,

Once again, we've rounded up the best romantic reading for you right here in Silhouette Intimate Moments. Start off with Maggie Shayne's *The Baddest Bride in Texas,* part of her top-selling miniseries THE TEXAS BRAND, and you'll see what I mean. Secrets, steam and romance...this book has everything.

And how many of you have been following that baby? A lot, I'll bet. And this month our FOLLOW THAT BABY cross-line miniseries concludes with *The Mercenary and the New Mom,* by Merline Lovelace. At last the baby's found—and there's romance in the air, as well.

If Western loving's your thing, we've got a trio of books to keep you happy. *Home Is Where the Cowboy Is,* by Doreen Roberts, launches a terrific new miniseries called RODEO MEN. THE SULLIVAN BROTHERS continue their wickedly sexy ways in *Heartbreak Ranch,* by Kylie Brant. And Cheryl Biggs's *The Cowboy She Never Forgot*—a book *you'll* find totally memorable—sports our WAY OUT WEST flash. Then complete your month's reading with *Suddenly a Family,* by Leann Harris. This FAMILIES ARE FOREVER title features an adorable set of twins, their delicious dad and the woman who captures all three of their hearts.

Enjoy them all—then come back next month for six more wonderful Intimate Moments novels, the most exciting romantic reading around.

Yours,

Leslie J. Wainger
Executive Senior Editor

Please address questions and book requests to:
Silhouette Reader Service
U.S.: 3010 Walden Ave., P.O. Box 1325, Buffalo, NY 14269
Canadian: P.O. Box 609, Fort Erie, Ont. L2A 5X3

Merline Lovelace

THE MERCENARY AND THE NEW MOM

Silhouette®

INTIMATE™ MOMENTS®

Published by Silhouette Books

America's Publisher of Contemporary Romance

Special thanks and acknowledgment to Merline Lovelace
for her contribution to the Follow That Baby miniseries.

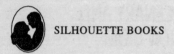 SILHOUETTE BOOKS

ISBN 0-373-07908-7

THE MERCENARY AND THE NEW MOM

Printed in U.S.A.

Books by Merline Lovelace

Silhouette Intimate Moments

Somewhere in Time #593
Night of the Jaguar #637
The Cowboy and the Cossack #657
Undercover Man #669
Perfect Double #692
†*The 14th...and Forever* #764
Return to Sender #866
If a Man Answers #878
The Mercenary and the New Mom #908

Silhouette Desire

Dreams and Schemes #872
†*Halloween Honeymoon* #1030
†*Wrong Bride, Right Groom* #1037

Silhouette Books

Fortune's Children

Beauty and the Bodyguard

*Code Name: Danger
†Holiday Honeymoons

MERLINE LOVELACE

After an exciting career as an air force officer, Merline Lovelace hung up her uniform and started writing romances. When not glued to her keyboard, Merline and her handsome hero, Al, enjoy golf, traveling and each other.

Merline enjoys hearing from readers, and can be reached at P.O. Box 892717, Oklahoma City, OK, 73189.

And watch for her next book, *Undercover Groom,* another sizzler about the fabulous Fortune family, coming from Silhouette Desire in June.

This one's for Gail and Leslie and all the folks at Silhouette who make murder and mayhem and breathtaking romantic suspense such fun!

Prologue

Sabrina Jensen would never know what pulled her from her light doze that cold, foggy March afternoon.

It could have been the heightened instincts of a new mom, still on constant red alert to the slightest sound from the newborn napping in the hooded white wicker bassinet.

It could have been the sense of danger that had dogged Sabrina day and night for the past several months. The danger that had kept her on the run, alone and pregnant and increasingly desperate, until finally she'd been forced to accept help from the family of the man she'd loved and lost so many months ago. The same family she'd believed wanted to take her baby from her.

Whatever woke her, Sabrina's gaze went instantly

to the bassinet she'd rolled into the toasty-warm living room of the luxurious guest cottage. Still nervous, still frightened for her baby even here, on the heavily guarded grounds of the Wentworth estate, she'd wanted her three-week-old infant near her while she tried to absorb the intricacies of Advanced Marketing Statistics.

When Sabrina saw the bassinet's snowy white outline in the dim shadows and heard no fretful sounds from the infant tucked inside, the fear gripping her heart eased. She was safe here. At last, she'd found sanctuary. Tomorrow, her baby would be christened. Everyone was coming tonight for dinner, and would stay over for the ceremony.

Everyone except the baby's father.

Aching with the constant sense of loss she carried tucked just under her heart, Sabrina felt the need to touch her baby. To brush a knuckle down the sleeping child's feather-soft cheek. Tossing aside a fleecy orange-and-black Oklahoma State University throw, she started to push herself off the leather sofa placed to catch both light and warmth from the fire in the stone fireplace. Her statistics textbook tumbled off her lap and hit the colorful, braided rag rug with a thud.

The noise caused a small movement in the shadows. The stir was so slight, so instantly stilled, that Sabrina almost missed it. She blinked once more to clear the last of the sleepy haze from her eyes. This time, her gaze penetrated the gloom beyond the heirloom wicker basket that held her baby.

Shock froze her where she stood. Her chest squeezed. She felt a single instant of pure joy.

"Jack!"

At her strangled gasp, the gaunt, bearded figure in the shadows turned his head. Slowly, so slowly, his mouth twisted into a travesty of the smile that had melted her bones the first time she saw it.

"Well, well. Sleeping Beauty wakes."

It was the Oklahoma drawl she remembered all too well. Husky. Masculine. As soft and as tough as rainwater on rawhide.

"And without a kiss from her prince," he added in a low growl.

His words evoked a memory that sent sharp, stinging hurt piercing into every inch of Sabrina's skin. The pain needled right through the terror that was rushing in to replace her brief, soaring instant of joy. He'd said those same words to her before, the day they'd met. The agony of hearing them again after so many months of heartache almost tore her apart.

Even greater than her agony, however, was her fear for her baby. Her whole body shaking, Sabrina pushed herself off the couch and faced the man she'd tumbled headlong into love with a short lifetime ago.

"You don't..." Her throat tight and aching, she forced out the same response she'd given him then. "You don't look much like a prince."

"I guess we've both learned that appearances can be deceiving."

A sudden wave of terror gripped her as Jack stepped around the bassinet and into the light. With his skin stretched tight across his cheekbones and his face stubbled with a rough, straggly beard, he looked as though he'd traveled to hell and back.

He had! She saw it in his eyes. Heard it in his voice.

Oh, God! How could she ache for him? How could she want to throw herself into his arms, and at the same time feel her fingers curling into claws at the thought of his hands on her body? How could he raise a flood of heat in her belly with that twisted smile, even as she furtively searched the shadowy living room for her purse with its concealed handgun?

As if sensing her rising panic, he halted a few steps away. The firelight glinted on his tobacco brown hair, once so short and neat, despite its stubborn tendency to curl when Sabrina ran her fingers through it.

Desperately, she inched sideways. Away from the bassinet. Toward the gun she'd bought after the first attempt on her life.

"They said…" She wet her lips. In a ragged whisper, she begged him to understand what she'd done. What she had to do to protect her child. "They said you died when that offshore rig blew up."

His eyes went so hard Sabrina felt their slice where she stood. "There were times I wished I had."

A million questions crashed through her, but the months of fear she'd lived with, the desperation she'd experienced, winnowed them down to just a few.

"How could you…?" She fought to drag breath into her aching lungs. "How could you go off like that? How could you rush off to fight a battle that wasn't your own like...like some damned mercenary when I...when we...?''

"I came back, Sabrina." A muscle worked in the side of his face. "I promised you I would. I made the same promise the day I met you."

"I remember," she whispered. "I remember."

Blue eyes locked with green. For a brief, searing moment, hostility, suspicion and fear receded. For that instant, they weren't standing in a room filled with the shadows of a wet March afternoon.

Almost, Sabrina could feel the heat of an early June sun on her upturned face. Almost, she could smell the riot of wild honeysuckle. Hear the screech of metal on metal as the oil pump in the field next to the Route 66 Diner shrieked its irritating, rhythmic song...

Chapter 1

With a bone-deep sigh, Sabrina propped her sneakered feet against a stack of empty wooden crates. A push of her toes tipped her fan-backed iron lawn chair against the wall. Lazily, she tilted her face to the warm June sun. The tantalizing scents of wild honeysuckle and fried onions teased her senses. Even after a year and a half of waitressing at the Route 66 Diner a half hour from Tulsa, Hank's onion-smothered chicken-fried steak could still make her mouth water.

Behind her, the diner's fitful air conditioner muttered and spit. The ancient unit kept the customers comfortable enough, but it couldn't battle the heat in the kitchen or the perspiration that had filmed Sabrina's temples as she'd thrown orders together for the breakfast rush. This morning's crowd had kept her hopping. The noon mob had been even worse...or better, depending on whether she considered her aching feet or how much today's crowd had added to the register take.

The noontime stream of truckers and locals had finally dwindled to a trickle. Sabrina had left the latecomers to Peg, the dark-eyed, imperturbable quarter Cherokee who'd taught Sabrina the ropes when she'd first started at the diner, and to her boss, who served as chief cook and wisecracking counselor to the truckers who'd made the diner a regular stop. With Hank's ribald advice to the lovelorn bluing the air, she'd sneaked out back for her first break since flicking on the pink neon Open sign at five-thirty this morning.

Raising her arms above her head, she wiggled and waved them a few times to work the kinks from her shoulders, then crossed her wrists on top of her loosely piled dark brown hair. The sun caught the patch of tummy between her jeans and white knit top bared by her lazy stretch. Smiling, Sabrina lifted her face another few degrees to drink in the sunshine. Surprisingly, the late afternoon heat soothed her instead of adding to her layers of gritty fatigue. By some magical alchemy, the warmth transformed her weariness into mere lethargy.

She closed her eyes, drowsing like a cat in the sun's rays. She might even have snatched a little snooze if not for the blasted oil well in the alfalfa field behind the diner. The walking arm on the pump had been screeching like a witch with her broom on fire since yesterday morning. Inside the diner, the nerve-scratching noise carried even over the raucous chatter of the patrons and the blare of the jukebox. Outside, it totally destroyed the peace of Sabrina's private little sanctuary. She'd stood it as long as she could yesterday, then called Wentworth Oil Works headquarters in Tulsa to complain. They'd promised to send a crew out as soon as possible.

As soon as possible had better be pretty darn quick, she thought, wincing as the metal arm took another, earsplitting plunge, then scraped upward. With a conscious effort of will, she blanked the irritating shriek from her mind. Like water pouring into a well, a host of other thoughts gushed in to fill the void.

She should be studying, not idling lazily in the sun, she thought with a little niggle of guilt. She had an accounting test tomorrow. Lord, she'd be glad when she finally finished her business degree. Only one more semester to go after this one, thank goodness. Between studying, waitressing, trying to make sense of Hank's casual approach to bookkeeping, hunting down antiques for the diner she was slowly transforming into an authentic Route 66 landmark, and taking care of Pop when his cross-country hauls brought him through Oklahoma, her cup runneth over.

At moments like this, though, the long shifts and late nights were worth all the effort she put into them. After a childhood spent drifting with her truck-driving father and twin sister, Sabrina had finally found her niche. More by chance than by choice, she'd enrolled at Oklahoma State University some years ago. Since then, she'd come to love the green, rolling hills of eastern Oklahoma almost as much as the warmhearted people who populated them. She'd worked several part-time jobs to pay for her college tuition before she started slinging hamburgers and chili at the Route 66 Diner.

Smiling, Sabrina remembered how the forties era relic had tugged at her imagination the first moment she'd spotted it from I-44. On impulse, she'd pulled off the interstate onto a narrow, two-lane access road. A brown-and-white historical marker proclaimed that this stretch of road had been part of the old Route 66, which once ran for 2,400 miles in an unbroken ribbon of asphalt from Chicago to Santa Monica, California. The diner named for the famous highway looked like a squat, round-shaped hut with a conical roof. Its fly-specked neon sign tipped at an angle over the front entrance, giving the entire establishment a lopsided look. Despite its ramshackle exterior, it had a charm and a history that instantly appealed to a woman who'd grown up on the road.

Once inside the place, Sabrina had been hooked. With no roots to the past herself, she'd delighted in the dented chrome counter stools, the shabby leatherette booths, even the broken-down jukebox that recalled a bygone era. On impulse, she'd plucked the hand-lettered Help Wanted sign out of the window and had been working with Hank and Peg ever since.

Bit by bit, she'd wheedled and argued and cajoled her boss into fixing up the old eatery. If everything went as planned, she'd buy it from Hank when he retired next year. She'd already submitted a small business loan preapproval package for review. If the loan went through, maybe, just maybe, the Route 66 Diner would become the first of a string of restored restaurants along the famous highway once known as America's Main Street.

Her dreams danced tantalizingly close, mingling with the sizzle of fried onions and the rumble of an eighteen-wheeler pulling out of the parking lot. Sabrina arched her back in another long, lazy stretch. She was still spinning out her particular vision of the future when the sun's warmth was suddenly cut off. Frowning, she opened her eyes.

"Well, well," a hazy shadow drawled. "Sleeping Beauty wakes."

Narrowing her eyes against the sun, Sabrina squinted at the stranger smiling down at her. His grin was pure, rogue male.

"And here I was hoping she'd need a kiss from her prince."

At the glint in his blue eyes, her stomach gave a queer little lurch that had nothing to do with the brimming bowl of Hank's supercharged chili she'd gulped down on the run a couple of hours ago. Dropping her arms, she cocked her head and looked the stranger over from the toes of his dusty boots to his blue denim shirt to the black ball cap with the Wentworth Oil logo on its crown.

"You don't look much like a prince to me," Sabrina tossed back. Her glance took in his partner standing beside a dusty red pickup. "Either of you," she amended.

Tall, lean and swarthy, the second man gave her a smile that lifted his well-groomed black mustache to reveal startlingly white teeth. But it was the blue-eyed charmer who responded to Sabrina's remark. His grin widening, he shot a quick glance at his partner. When he turned back, his eyes were filled with laughter.

"Appearances can be deceiving, sweetheart."

The lurch her stomach had taken a few seconds ago was nothing to the wild somersault it now performed. Good grief! This lean-hipped, jean-clad roustabout ought to come with a warning label!

Dangerous when smiling.

Dangerous even when not smiling, Sabrina suspected wryly. His kind always were. She had only the haziest memory of the too handsome bull rider her mother had run off with when she and her sister were toddlers. If Sabrina had to guess, she'd bet the rodeo cowboy had oozed the same outrageous sex appeal as this broad-shouldered hunk.

Her sneakers slid off the stack of wooden crates. The iron lawn chair hit the porch with a thump. Pushing out of the chair, Sabrina tucked a straggling tendril of her shoulder-length sable hair behind one ear. She hadn't heard these guys drive up, which wasn't surprising considering the roar of the semi that had pulled out of the lot and the shrieking pump a few yards away.

Thank goodness relief was at hand.

"It's about time you guys got here. I was just

thinking about making another call to Wentworth Oil. This one wouldn't have been as polite as the last.''

The stranger thumbed back his ball cap, revealing a shock of short brown hair a few shades lighter than her own. ''Is that right?''

''Think you can fix it?''

Older and wiser, Peg would have termed the look he gave her as pure-dy devil.

''I can fix anything, sweetheart.''

''You can drop the 'sweetheart' bit,'' Sabrina said tartly. ''It's beginning to grate almost as much as your darned pump.''

He followed her annoyed glance to the oil rig. The black pump head rode up on the walking arm, then plunged down again, like a giant grasshopper bobbing in an alfalfa crop. A particularly loud grind of metal on metal made Sabrina wince.

''It's been screeching like that since yesterday morning, annoying the customers and driving me nuts.''

''Such a noise would drive me to nuts as well,'' the black-haired, mustachioed roustabout standing beside the truck added with a grimace.

Sabrina blinked at his odd phrasing. She couldn't quite place his accent. He certainly didn't hail from around these parts. Mexico, she guessed. Or perhaps from some place farther south. A good number of workers from the Venezuelan oil fields had migrated to Oklahoma and Texas in recent years.

Hands on hips, she looked from him to his partner. ''Well, are you two going to get to work or not?''

They exchanged one of those male kinds of looks that could have meant anything from "Let's have a cold beer first" to "Where'd this one come from?"

"I guess we are, sweet—er...Miss...?"

"Jensen. Sabrina Jensen."

The blue-eyed hunk tipped his ball cap. "I'm Jack, and this is my friend...Al."

The swarthy oil worker bowed from the waist. The gesture looked so ridiculous in the diner's dusty back parking lot, and so astonishingly graceful, that Sabrina had to smile.

"Pleasure meeting you, Al. You too, Jack. Now, you two had better fix that thing before we're all permanently hearing impaired."

"Yes, ma'am."

Hiding a grin, Jack Wentworth strolled back to the pickup where Ali Fashor Kaisal waited patiently, twirling one tip of his mustache.

"I promised to show you some of back-road Oklahoma on the way to the airport in Tulsa," Jack said, "but I didn't intend to put you to work. This might delay your departure for a while."

"It is my plane," Ali replied with a careless shrug. "It does not depart until I say it does."

"So, what do you think? Do you remember how to take an oil rig apart and put it back together again?"

"Ah, my friend, some things one never forgets."

Grinning, the CEO of Wentworth Oil Works and the Crown Prince of the Royal House of Qatar stripped off their shirts. Jack tossed his carelessly in the truck bed. With the ingrained courtesy of the East, Ali carefully folded the shirt that he'd borrowed from his old friend along with jeans and a well-creased straw Stetson.

The warmth of the sun on Jack's back felt good, damned good. Almost as good as the prospect of working side by side with Ali again. More years than he wanted to count had passed since the first time he and the prince, then the disgraced younger son of the Emir of Qatar, had sweated together in the sheikdom's rich oil fields. In the years since, Ali had become heir to one of the world's richest sheikdoms after his older brother's death, and Jack had moved up the corporate ladder at Wentworth Oil Works, but he knew darn well that neither one of them had forgotten the basic skills they'd learned under the blistering sun. The skills that formed their common heritage.

"From the sound of it, I'd say the head joint on the walking arm has frozen up."

"It sounds so to me, also."

Rummaging in the storage compartment in the truck bed, Jack pulled out a toolbox. Good thing he'd taken a company vehicle when he'd offered Ali this impromptu tour of Oklahoma.

"Should be a piece of cake to fix."

"But not too much of this cake." Ali slanted a glance at the woman watching them from the back of the diner, one palm raised to shade her eyes from the glare. "It does not hurt to impress the so beautiful Sabrina with our prowess, no?"

"Careful, Kaisal," Jack warned. "The last time you and Hatmir met me for dinner in Paris, she swore she'd make a eunuch of you if you strayed again."

"She is much a woman, my Hatmir. But so, I think, is this one."

Jack thought so too, but he wasn't about to admit it to the Playboy of the Middle East. As rich as he was powerful in the world of petro-politics, the Crown Prince of Qatar made a hobby of collecting beautiful women...and Sabrina Jensen certainly fell into that category.

Jack stole another assessing look himself, only to catch her doing the same. Unconsciously, he puffed out his chest and hollowed his stomach. Just a little. He'd worked enough years in the oil fields and on offshore rigs to burn every ounce of fat from his body. He kept himself in shape even now, despite the fact that he spent most of his time hustling corporate mergers and international consortiums instead of twenty-foot lengths of pipe. He wouldn't win any Mr. America contests, but it didn't hurt his ego a bit to catch the delectable Ms. Jensen eyeing him with a hint of interest in her luminous green eyes.

At that moment, she noticed him noticing her noticing him. With a flush, she swept back another wayward strand of brown hair so dark it appeared almost black.

"I have to get back to work."

He barely caught her embarrassed mutter over the

noise of the pump, but he couldn't miss the heat staining her cheeks. Spinning around on one sneaker, she
retreated inside the diner. The rear view, Jack decided, proved as exceptional as the front. No doubt
about it, Sabrina Jensen was trophy quality.

Dozing in the sun like a sleek, lazy cat, the woman
had just about tied him up in knots. With her arms
crossed atop her pile of dark hair and that slice of
bare midriff peeking up at him, she'd made his throat
go dry and dusty as a played-out well.

Then she'd opened those striking green eyes.

Jack was as much of a sucker as the prince for long
legs and the firm, full breasts outlined so deliciously
under Sabrina Jensen's knit top. When they came
packaged with the keen intelligence he'd glimpsed in
her eyes and a mouth that stopped just short of sin,
he'd decided on the spot to drive back this way after
he'd delivered Ali to the entourage waiting with his
private jet.

Damn! The entourage! Jack shook his head, thinking about the State Department representative who'd
flown in with the prince's entourage.

"I'd better call Trey and let him know we'll be
delayed. He tends to get nervous about things like
security and schedules."

Ali shrugged. "That one, he is always nervous."

He didn't used to be, Jack thought as he reached
inside the pickup's cab for the mobile phone. The
consummate State Department official, Trey McGill
had set up a good number of the clandestine missions
Jack had carried out for the government over the past

ten years. Trey's extensive experience had proved extraordinarily useful, although it was Jack's own far-flung business and oil contacts that had provided his cover and his access to spots where most Americans weren't welcome. He and Trey made a good team—or they had until Heather.

Jack's fingers fisted on the cell phone. Even now, two years after Heather Blake's accidental death, guilt stabbed at him. It didn't matter that he hadn't known Trey had a thing for the blond, ambitious Washington D.C. lawyer. Or that she'd dropped McGill like a hot brick when he'd introduced her to the Oklahoma oil executive. Heather's excessive drinking and stubborn reliance on pills had killed their brief affair almost before it got started, but she'd somehow convinced herself that Jack intended to marry her. At least, that was what she'd sobbed to Trey the night she OD'ed. Jack had been in South America on a mission then. Stonefaced, McGill had given him the news when he returned.

Two years, and the guilt still ate at Jack's conscience. Two years, and he hadn't been able to bridge the yawning gap between himself and the man he shared so many missions and tense hours with. Blowing out a long breath, he punched in Trey's number and his own ID code.

The State Department rep answered on the first ring. "Where the hell are you?"

"At a diner along a stretch of old Route 66, about fifteen miles outside Tulsa."

"A diner? The prince's staff has a banquet ready

to serve as soon as they take off, and you stop at a diner?'' His voice sharpened. ''What's that noise in the background? What's going on?''

''Relax, Trey. Nothing's going on. That's a rusty walking arm you hear.''

''A what?''

''Never mind. Look, tell the aircrew to hang loose. We'll be there in a couple of hours.''

''A couple of hours! It doesn't take that long to travel fifteen miles.''

''We're taking a break for a cool one.''

Which they would, as soon as they freed up and lubricated the pump head.

''Dammit, Wentworth, you know we had to get special clearance from Customs to bring the prince's aircraft into Tulsa. It's sitting on the runway in plain sight, a nice, juicy target for any nut with a grudge against Middle Easterners. I've got two dozen security folks sweating blood every extra minute this baby is on the ground.''

Jack didn't remind Trey that the State Department had suggested bringing the prince to Oklahoma in the first place. Using the cover of the endowment of a multimillion dollar energy research facility at OSU funded jointly by Wentworth Oil and the Sheikdom of Qatar, Jack and Ali had met secretly to go over the details of a new Arabian Peninsula accord proposed by the U.S. Ali was carrying the draft accord back to his father. Hopefully, the emir would agree to its content, if not its exact wording, and present the draft to the other powerful leaders who controlled the flow of oil out of the Persian Gulf. With the political situation so unstable in that region, all parties agreed that it was best to keep the negotiations secret until the accord was a done deal.

"I'll let you know when we hit the road," Jack assured the agitated rep.

Flipping the cell phone shut on Trey's protest, he joined Ali at the back of the truck.

"Ready to wrestle with some rusted iron?"

Ali's white teeth flashed under his mustache. "I am ready, my friend."

It took them exactly forty minutes to shut down the pump, remove the head casing, chip the rust from the main joint, and lubricate every moving part. Using sheer muscle power, they tested the up-and-down motion of the walking arm for resistance. The metal rod moved smoothly...and noiselessly, thank God. Grunting, they manhandled the casing back into place and took turns wrenching the bolts down tight.

By the time they finished, sweat ran down Jack's back. Ali's mustache drooped at the corners and dripped in the center. Black grease and Oklahoma red dust streaked their arms and chests.

Jack dropped the tools back in the box and tossed Ali a dispenser of the dry soap and the clean rags that no oilman's truck was ever without. "Nice work for a man who hasn't bent a wrench in twenty years."

"Ha! And you have, my friend?" Ali scrubbed the grime from his chest and arms. "Since your grandfather makes you chief operating officer of Wentworth Oil, you do nothing but complain about the paperwork and the meetings. I think that is why you undertake these so dangerous trips for your government. You crave the excitement we once found in the oil fields.''

"Maybe. What I crave right now, though, is something long, liquid and icy cold. Hey, save me some of that stuff. I can't go inside looking like this."

Ali tossed him the dry soap and dragged on his shirt. "That is, as you say, your problem. I shall go for you, yes?''

"No!"

"Don't worry. I shall give the so beautiful Sabrina your order for something cold.'' His black eyes gleamed. "And I, my friend, shall ask for something hot.''

With a tip of his borrowed straw Stetson, he left Jack cursing and furiously scrubbing his arms and chest.

Chapter 2

Dammit!

Shoving his shirttails into his jeans, Jack strode through the dusty parking lot toward the front of the flat-roofed, stucco diner. He should have known better than to let Ali have first crack at the soap and rags. Put him within a five-mile radius of a woman like Sabrina Jensen and the prince was like a hound with the scent of a doe up. If Jack didn't watch it, he'd end up delivering two people to that plane in Tulsa…and Hatmir would have him for lunch the next time he was in Qatar.

Even more to the point, he wanted to try his luck with the delectable Ms. Jensen himself.

He followed the curve of round, squatty building to the front door. Above the few steps leading to the door, a peeling neon sign right out of the forties flashed the diner's name and Good Eats in pink and faded turquoise. It was the kind of place that had dotted the roads during Route 66's heyday. The kind of place that still catered to a crowd more interested in good food than fancy decor.

Jack pushed through the diner's heavy glass door, intent on defusing the million-watt charm Ali could turn on and off like a flashlight. Just inside the door, he stopped short, astounded. For an eerie moment, Jack wondered if he'd gone back in time.

Shiny chrome, bright neon advertisements and pink leatherette seat covers screamed for attention, vying with the scrubbed and spotless black-and-white tile floor. Perry Como crooned from a massive Wurlitzer jukebox. Posters advertising chrome-laden Pontiacs and wood-sided Ford station wagons decorated the walls. Pool balls clattered in a smoky room off to one side, and truck drivers hunched over a gray-speckled Formica counter, wolfing down coffee and pie.

Even more distracting were the mouthwatering aromas of fried onions and chili. Suddenly ravenous, Jack wove a path through the tables and joined Ali at the counter. His friend, he noted, hadn't wasted any time. A half-devoured slice of banana cream pie sat before him.

"You must try this," the prince exclaimed between forkfuls. "It is most wonderful."

Straddling one of the round stools, Jack decided he didn't want pie. He wanted a cold beer, a plateful of whatever was sizzling on the grill, and a few words

with the woman in the kitchen. He could see her in
the pass-through window dividing the counter area
from the grill. Tendrils of dark hair lay in damp,
feathery curls on her neck. Her white knit tank top
clung to her body. With smooth efficiency, she
wrapped the strings of a white apron twice around her
slim waist and nudged aside the balding, barrel-
chested cook.

"You need a break, Hank."

"I'm fine."

"Go on, get off your feet for a while."

The cook scowled around the unlit black cigar
clamped between his teeth.

"Bossy females. Between you and Peg, a man
can't chew, can't spit, can't smoke, can't even call
his kitchen his own."

Sabrina plucked the spatula from his fist. "You
know the doc said you had to give those varicose
veins a rest. Now, scoot!"

Grumbling, the cook left her to man the grill. An
expert flip of the spatula turned a heap of succulent,
golden brown onions. Another flip and a hard press
squeezed jets of fat from a juicy hamburger. Jack
hadn't seen one that big or that thick since his high
school days. Saliva rushed into his mouth.

Wielding the spatula with brisk competence, Sabrina called to him through the window. "You and
your friend did a good job on that rig. I can hear
myself think for the first time in two days."

"If you have any more problems, call Wentworth
Oil."

"Ask for Jack," Ali added with a wicked wink at the waitress. "This one, he needs the hard work to keep him from trouble."

"I can believe that," she retorted. "What'll you have, Jack?"

"One of those hamburgers. With lots of onions. And a cold beer."

"Sorry. We gave up our liquor license a few months back. Iced tea okay?"

"Fine."

"Damned bossy females." The ousted cook settled on the stool beside Jack. "Just because some truckers got pie-faced and tore up the place a time or two, Sabrina decided we shouldn't serve beer anymore."

Jack swept another glance around the gleaming diner. "Guess I can't blame her. This place is a gem."

The cook snorted. "When I bought it thirty years ago, it was a dive. It would *still* be a dive if Sabrina Jensen hadn't waltzed in one afternoon and told me she was going to be my new waitress. Don't know where she keeps digging up those old posters and all this…this stuff."

"This is her doing?"

"All of it." Hank's gray brows tipped into a scowl under his shiny bald pate. "The tiles on the floor, these stools, even the dang-blasted music. That's one managing female."

"So I noticed."

She'd certainly put Jack and Ali to work fast enough.

"Next thing you know, she'll be tellin' me to water down my chili just 'cause it gave a couple of pansy-assed tourists the trots."

For all his grumbling, Hank's eyes turned sharp with worry when his employee arched her back and swiped a wrist across her brow.

"Fool woman's determined to work herself to death. I told her I'd sell her the place cheap, but she keeps insistin' I need a hefty down payment for my retirement fund." He huffed. "Hell, my wife'll probably kill me within a week of havin' me underfoot, so what do I need with a retirement fund?"

"Beats me," Jack agreed companionably.

Still grumbling, Hank crossed his arms on the gray Formica counter. His right forearm sported a tattooed anchor and chain. The left, a heart entwined with either vines or snakes. Given the way his skin wrinkled and sagged, it was hard to tell which.

Smiling, Jack took in the decorations. "What ship did you serve on?"

"The *Jefferson*. Leakingest coal bucket in the U.S. Navy."

"True, but she did us proud at Midway."

Hank sat up straighter. "That she did. I was chief cook's mate during that little skirmish in the Pacific." He gave Jack a keen look. "What about you? When did you serve?"

"I pulled a hitch as a SEABEE after college."

"That so?" The cook rolled his fat black cigar to the other side of his mouth and stuck out a hairy paw.

"I'm Hank. Hank Donovan. Always glad to have another sailor drop anchor at the diner."

"I'm Jack. This is my friend Al."

While Ali shook hands with the stubby restaurateur, Jack thought back to his navy career. It seemed like a lifetime ago. It was, he reflected with a rueful grimace.

The grandson of crusty old Joseph Wentworth, one of Oklahoma's original oil barons, Jack had spent his boyhood summers as a roustabout in the oil fields and eighteen long months following high school graduation as a tool pusher on an offshore rig in the frigid North Sea. After finishing a degree in petroleum engineering at the University of Oklahoma, he'd decided to try his hand at something other than the family business.

To his disappointment, the navy had jumped on his offshore drilling expertise. They'd put him in command of an elite underwater construction and demolition unit. As it turned out, Jack had thrived on the excitement and danger inherent in the underwater operations, but he'd left the navy after his grandfather's first stroke and joined Wentworth Oil. In the years since, he'd worked his way up the corporate ladder to CEO.

He was good at what he did. Very good. Wentworth Oil Works was now a multinational conglomerate with interests in every corner of the world. Still, Jack had been feeling restless and caged when a friend in the State Department asked him to use his far-flung contacts in the oil world to conduct a "special" negotiation for the U.S.

That request had led to another, even more secret mission, then another. Now, the intermittent undercover operations provided Jack with the risk and excitement he missed in the corporate world. The dangerous missions and extended travel also demanded that he keep his relationships with women light and unentangling…as he'd learned the hard way with Heather.

Which didn't keep his pulse from kicking into overdrive when Sabrina Jensen pushed through the swinging door from the kitchen with what looked like a quart-size glass of iced tea in each hand.

"It's already sweetened," she warned, plunking the tea down.

Smiling his thanks, Jack lifted the glass just as Sabrina turned and bent to retrieve napkins and silverware from a shelf under the pass-through window. He almost choked on his tea.

Had he considered her rear view merely exceptional? He must have been blind. She had the sexiest tush and sweetest, curving thighs he'd ever seen!

Evidently Ali thought so, too. The prince's fork had frozen halfway to his mouth. Bits of cream decorated his mustache. His black eyes gleamed with an avaricious light. One that Jack had seen too many times in the past.

Lowering his glass, he thumped Ali on the back. Hard. "Guess you'll be glad to see Hatmir and the kids, buddy. What's it been, two weeks?"

No fool, Ali knew exactly what Jack was up to.

"Two weeks," he concurred with a bland smile. "It is good that I am Muslim and so rich from the oil fields, no? I have but one wife, but the Koran allows me to take more if I can support them."

On Jack's other side, Hank puffed out his cheeks. "It don't matter how much money a man's got in the bank, he can't afford more'n one wife. She'll drain him dry, one way or another!"

"What about you?" Amused, Sabrina laid napkins and silverware on the counter in front of Jack. "How many wives do you have?"

"None." At her skeptical look, he held up a palm. "Not one, I swear."

"He is too slippery, this one." With a gleeful grin, Ali returned Jack's hearty thump on the back. "I have known him for many years. He chases the women most diligently, but he does not let them catch him. He has left many broken hearts behind him."

The prince's banter sent another barb of guilt through Jack. Ali didn't know about Heather. Few did, outside of Trey McGill.

"Somehow," Sabrina drawled, "I'm not surprised."

She sailed back into the kitchen, leaving the oilman to scowl at the prince. "Thanks a lot, buddy."

"You are most welcome…buddy."

Their semigood-natured rivalry heated up when Sabrina returned with a heaping platter. A huge hamburger lapped the edges of the plate. A mountain of onions sat atop the meat patty. Ripe red tomatoes, crisp lettuce, a long wedge of dill and mounds of crisp, greasy french fries filled the rest of the platter.

Having finished his pie, Ali waited until Jack had wrapped both hands around his burger and taken a man-size bite before proceeding to tell Sabrina about the fabulous riches that would be hers if she left her apron behind and flew off to Qatar with him.

"I shall drape you in silks," he promised. "Cover you with pearls. No, no, it must be emeralds, to match your so beauteous eyes."

"Right," she laughed. "Emeralds."

"You shall have your own house, and a yacht. We no longer keep the harem, you understand." Real regret seemed to pass across his face. He shook it off. "Although you must wear the chador in public, you will be free to come and go as you please."

"Don't listen to him," Jack warned between great, satisfying bites. "He keeps Hatmir on an even shorter leash than she keeps him."

"You wound me, my friend. Sabrina must know that if she comes away with me, I shall lay all the treasures of the East at her feet."

"All I know is that you two make even more noise than that rig did."

Folding her arms, she rested her hips against the back counter. Laughter gleamed in her eyes. Her full mouth curved in a smile. She had no idea that Ali was serious, Jack thought wryly. With all the truckers frequenting this place, she probably received even more extravagant offers every day. If she only knew it, this one could change her life forever.

For a moment, he toyed with the idea of introducing himself and the prince. As quickly as the thought occurred, he quashed it. If Ali couldn't woo Sabrina with his promises of riches, that was his friend's tough luck. Jack, on the other hand, operated better without an audience watching his every move. He wolfed down the rest of his hamburger with the same gusto as the other patrons, then tried to hustle his friend away.

Ali wouldn't budge.

"No, no. I must have another piece of this so delicious pie." His playboy's smile flashed. "And more conversation with the beauteous Sabrina."

Shaking her head at his flattery, she slid another generous wedge onto his plate.

"The pie will cost you a buck-fifty. The conversation will have to wait. There's a bushel of okra waiting to be cleaned for tonight's special."

With a glance at the antique Coca-Cola clock above the counter, she pushed through the door to the kitchen once more.

"What is this okra?" Ali asked the room at large.

Hank slid off his stool. "After I get done stewin' it in Tabasco and red peppers, it's heaven and hell in one bowl."

Rolling his fat, unlit stogie around in his mouth, he followed Sabrina into the kitchen.

The prince's mustache twitched. "We must stay to try this heavenly, hellish dish."

"We can't. Your crew is waiting for you, remember? So is McGill."

Ali dismissed a crew of six, another half-dozen security and communications personnel, an augmentee team from the State Department, and Trey McGill with a shrug of one muscled shoulder.

"So, they wait."

Damn! Jack hadn't intended to spin this little interlude out for more than an hour or so. Certainly not for the length of time it would take Hank to stew up a fresh batch of okra. Trey's ulcer would be spitting fire if they delayed that long.

Despite his best efforts, however, he couldn't convince the prince to abandon the field. While Jack looked on in mingled exasperation and amusement, Ali downed yet a third piece of pie and more coffee, dished up by an equally amused Sabrina.

Finally the stubborn Middle Easterner got his first taste of Hank's stewed okra. Ignoring Jack's suggestion that he crumble a chunk of corn bread in the bowl to absorb some of the fiery liquid, Ali scooped up a brimming spoonful and downed it with a jaunty flourish.

A second later, his cheeks hollowed. His eyes bugged. Beads of sweat popped out on his forehead. Dropping the spoon with a clatter, he snatched up the glass of water Sabrina had ready.

"That," he gasped, "is hotter even than the Great Desert of Qatar."

Downing the rest of the water in great, noisy gulps, he dragged his forearm across his soggy mustache. Jack gave him only enough time to douse the fires before grabbing the man's arm and pulling him off the stool.

"The Great Desert is where your father will send you if you don't haul your carcass out of here."

"But…"

Ali caught himself. As much as he enjoyed living up to his well-deserved reputation as jet-setting playboy, he'd inherited a burden of heavy responsibility upon the death of his older brother. Now Crown Prince and heir apparent, Ali Fashor Kaisal had learned to put his country's needs before his own.

"Yes," he said with a long, melodramatic sigh. "I must go."

Sabrina listened to the exchange with mounting amusement. What a couple of characters! Granted, they were handsome enough, each in his own way. The black-haired Al undoubtedly stopped more than one woman in her tracks with that flashing smile. She wondered how many gullible females took him up on his effusive offers to drape them in emeralds and pearls.

Yet it was the other one she couldn't quite seem to catch her breath around. Okay, that glimpse she'd caught of Jack stripped to the waist and bathed in bright sunlight had done serious damage to her respiratory system. And, yes, she felt a distinct flutter somewhere around the vicinity of her midsection whenever he turned those baby blues in her direction. But Sabrina had been around enough in her twenty-four years, first with her dad and sister, then on her own. She knew better than to go all gooey over a broad-shouldered, lean-hipped rigger who was here today and off to the next field tomorrow.

Particularly, she noted with a twist of her lips, broad-shouldered, lean-hipped riggers who didn't have enough cash to pay for their meals.

Frowning, Jack dug in his back pockets and came up empty-handed. He patted his front pockets, then tried the back again.

"I must have left my wallet in the truck."

Sure he did, Sabrina thought wryly as he turned to his friend.

"Do you have any cash on you?"

"Not U.S. dollars." Al's mustache lifted in a flashing smile. "Will you take Qatarian dinars, most beauteous Sabrina?"

Right. As if the local bank would exchange Qatarian dinars! For reasons she couldn't quite define, though, Sabrina didn't want Jack and his friend to lose face in front of Hank and the other patrons.

"Forget it," she told them with a cheerful smile. "That screeching oil rig's been driving us all nuts. Your meal's on the house."

Red tinged Jack's cheeks. "My wallet's in the truck," he said a little stiffly. "Hang on a second, I'll go get it."

He didn't like accepting a handout, Sabrina saw. Few of the down-and-outers who drifted into the diner did. Still, no one ever left the Route 66 Diner hungry. For all his grumbling and griping, Hank insisted on that. Her boss hid a serious soft streak under his gruff exterior, which was only one of the reasons Sabrina had stayed to work for him so long.

The blue-eyed rigger was back a few moments later. One glance at his crestfallen face told her he hadn't located his "missing" billfold.

Jack kept his expression sheepish with some effort. He'd found his leather wallet lying in the dust beside the truck. It had probably fallen out when he and Ali stripped down to work on the rig. He was halfway back to the diner, peeling out a fifty and planning to leave Sabrina a fat tip, when he'd realized that the unpaid bill provided him with the perfect excuse to swing back by the diner after getting rid of Ali.

His conscience nagged him a bit about letting Sabrina think he was broke. He probably wouldn't have kept up the subterfuge if he hadn't been thinking of Heather earlier. She hadn't tried to disguise the fact that his wealth attracted her as much as Jack himself did. The temptation to spend a few more hours with a woman who didn't see dollar signs every time she looked at him was too strong for Jack to resist.

"Sorry," he told the green-eyed waitress. "I'll have to owe you."

"Don't worry about it."

"I'll come back, Sabrina. I promise."

Laughing, she walked him and Ali to the door. "I know you tool pushers. I won't hold my breath."

Jack turned, letting the late afternoon heat waffle through the open glass door. With it came the sweet scent of the wild honeysuckle that grew over the fences all up and down Oklahoma's backroads. Smiling, he stared down at the woman who held the door with one hand and hooked the other on the waistband of her jeans. He slid a knuckle under her chin, tilting her head back.

"I'll be back."

For a moment, Sabrina thought he was going to kiss her. Right there in front of Hank and the small crowd of interested diners. For the same, breathless instant, she thought she was going to do something monumentally stupid…like let him. A sudden, urgent need to feel his mouth on hers whipped along her nerve endings. Her fingers curled on the metal door frame. She started to go up on tiptoe.

Then he dropped his hand, and she had to bite her lip to keep from letting her disappointment show on her face. She felt it, though. On every square inch of her skin.

By the time Jack sauntered down the steps and joined his partner for the walk back to the rear lot, her common sense had reasserted itself. The last thing she needed was to get tangled up with a down-at-the-heels roustabout, for heaven's sake. She didn't have the time. Or the energy!

The dinner crowd would start showing up in the next half hour or so. The supper rush would take almost all she had, yet she still needed to put in another few hours studying for her test when she got home. With her degree so darned close and ownership of the diner almost within grasp, she had to stay focused.

Sabrina took a deep breath, drawing in the heat and the sweet, almost overpowering scent from the vines

covering the fences across the road. Despite her determined pep talk, she had to tear her gaze away from
Jack's tight, neat buns and long-legged stride.

Sighing, she turned to go back to work. The door
had just started to swing shut behind her when the
sound of tires squealing ripped through the stillness.
Sabrina spun around just in time to see a battered
black pickup peel off the road and into the lot. To her
horror, it aimed straight for Jack and Al.

Chapter 3

"Jack! Al! Look out!"

Sabrina's scream got lost in the whine of the pickup's engine. Her heart in her throat, she watched in spiraling terror as the dust-covered black Ford careened across the parking lot toward the two men.

With a vicious curse, Jack shoved his friend aside. Al hit the ground rolling. The pickup zoomed by, missing him by mere inches.

Jack wasn't as lucky.

Just when it seemed a collision was inevitable, he leaped up and landed on the hood with a thud that stopped Sabrina's heart. In one of those terrifying instants that seemed to last two lifetimes, he rolled across the hood.

She couldn't breathe. Couldn't move. Couldn't

even scream. A distant corner of her mind recorded his amazing agility, marveling at the athletic way he landed on his feet on the other side of the fast-moving truck. At that moment, though, she couldn't appreciate anything but the fact that he'd avoided certain death.

She was almost sobbing with relief when the truck's brakes shrieked. Throwing up a cloud of dust and small rocks, the battered pickup fishtailed to a halt. A moment later, two men spilled out. So did an almost empty Jack Daniel's bottle. The glass shattered when it hit the ground, adding the smoky tang of Tennessee sippin' whiskey to the swirling dust.

It didn't take a rocket scientist to figure out the two men were as drunk as bar dogs on a Saturday night. One staggered as he walked. The other moved with the stiff, exaggerated gait of someone trying too hard to appear perfectly sober.

"You damned idiots," Jack snarled, dusting himself off. "You almost killed us."

The shorter of the two drew himself up. "Hey, who you callin' idiots? We wasn't the ones who walked in front of a movin' pickup."

The taller of the two men hooked his thumbs in his jeans and rocked back on his boot heels, measuring Jack from head to toe. Evidently he didn't like what he saw. His lip curled at one corner, and a malicious gleam entered his watery blue eyes.

"It looked to me like you danced outta the way easy enough, pretty boy."

"It looks to me," Al ground out, his black eyes

furious as he, too, dusted himself off, "that you are both most drunk and irresponsible."

"Listen to him!" The shorter man gave a snort that was part giggle, part belch. "He sure talks prissy, don't he, Sam?"

"He sure does, Digger."

Sabrina groaned. These two were drunk *and* spoiling for a fight. She'd seen their kind often enough, which was one of the reasons she'd finally convinced Hank to stop serving beer at the diner. She started forward, intending to defuse the situation, when a wide grin split the one called Digger's face, showing an empty space where his two lower front teeth had been.

"They're all duded up like cowboys or riggers, but I bet they never sat no bull or wrestled no pipe."

"Oh, you could be wrong there," his buddy drawled, rocking back on his worn boot heels once more. "That one there, he's Jack Wentworth."

Jack *Wentworth!*

Sabrina stopped short, her peace-making intentions forgotten. Incredulous, she swung around to stare at the rigger in the black ball cap. He didn't work for Wentworth Oil Works. He *was* Wentworth Oil Works! And Wentworth Shipping International. And Wentworth Bank and Trust…which just happened to be reviewing her preloan application package.

Her gasp brought Jack's head around, but only for a moment. The tall one, the one called Sam, pulled his attention back.

"I saw pretty boy and old Joe Wentworth workin'

a rig down Ardmore way a few years ago,'' he said with a sneer. ''They was both up to their elbows in grease. Course, some artsy-fartsy photographer was followin' them around at the time, takin' pictures for *Life* or something, so's it was probably all a pose.''

Another snigger from the shorter man took the tense situation and made it a whole lot worse.

''What do you say, Jackie boy? You want to pose for us? You and your Arab friend here? We know a couple of Texicans down 'round San Antonio who would surely enjoy some pictures of you two doin' the two-step, if you know what I mean.''

''Tell you what,'' Jack drawled. ''We'll take some pictures for those Texicans…of you two planted head down and ass up in that alfalfa field.''

''No, no, my friend.'' Al twirled one end of his mustache, his face bland as he looked the other two over. ''We must not despoil the earth with such foulness. We shall merely—how do you say?—grind them up and toss their ashes to the winds.''

Things were fast getting out of hand. Sabrina shook herself out of her immobility and pushed forward.

''Now just wait a minute. This is ridiculous. No one's going to grind anyone into…''

Her protest went unheeded as Jack flashed his friend a wide grin. ''Sounds good to me. You take the runt. I've got the ugly one.''

Before Sabrina could get out another word, Jack and Al launched themselves at the two troublemakers. All four went down in a chorus of grunts and a flurry of pummeling fists.

"Oh, for...!"

Sabrina threw up her hands. Men! She'd never met one yet who could walk away from an insult or a taunt. Okay, so maybe she couldn't respect a man who did, but there were other ways to settle disputes than rolling in the dust, pummeling each other. She glanced around, searching for some way to break up the free-for-all. At the side of the diner she spotted the hose Hank used to wash down the dusty parking lot whenever he remembered to get around to it. She was headed for the hose when the diner's front door thudded open. Customers piled out, one almost atop the other, drawn by the sounds of the fight.

"What's going on?" Hank demanded.

"A couple of drunks almost ran over Jack and Al. The four of them are discussing the matter now," Sabrina added dryly.

To her disgust, the diners cheered the combatants on. With a shake of her head, she marched over to the hose and twisted the spigot all the way to the right. Placing her thumb over the mouth to add to the water's force, Sabrina turned.

Before she could aim and shoot, the battle was over. Although the two drunks fought surprisingly well for men whose movements should have been impeded by the liquor they'd consumed, they both went down. A brutal right to the stomach from Al doubled over the one called Digger. He crumpled to the dirt. The taller one took a hard fist to the face and spun away from Jack. He crashed into his battered pickup. Flinging an arm over the side of the truck bed to steady himself, he hung there, panting and glaring. Blood gushed from his nose. A bruise was already forming on the side of his jaw.

Jack unclenched his fists and flexed his bruised knuckles. "You two better sober up before you hit the road…and before you decide to shoot your mouths off anymore."

The glare in Sam's eyes turned murderous. He grappled in the truck bed for a moment, then pushed himself away. This time, he didn't come at Jack with bare fists and bruised knuckles. This time, he clutched a length of steel pipe. Hank shouted a warning to Jack as the pipe swung in a deadly arc.

Without conscious thought, Sabrina whipped up the hose and aimed it. The pulsing stream hit Sam full in the face, throwing his swing off just enough to allow his intended victim to duck under the pipe. Jack sprang back up on a rush of what looked like pure adrenaline. Planting a blow to the ribs that gusted Sam's breath out on a whooshing grunt, he followed with a swift upper cut. His target staggered back one pace, then two. Then his knees buckled and he folded to the ground, wheezing like an old, anguished accordion.

Chest heaving, Jack kicked the pipe away and stood over him. A silence settled over the dusty parking lot. When Sam showed no inclination to continue the battle, the coiled tension in Jack's shoulders eased a fraction. A moment later, he spun on his heel. Striding over to where Sabrina stood, he swept an arm around her waist and brought her up against him, gushing hose and all.

"Thanks, sweetheart."

His face wore a coating of dust and sweat. Blood splattered his blue denim shirt. His heart still hammered with a force so fast and strong Sabrina could feel its erratic beat against her breasts. His blue eyes gleamed with the sheer thrill of a male who'd just claimed a neat and perfectly senseless victory.

Despite herself, Sabrina had to smile. "You're welcome."

Then he bent his head and kissed her. She saw it coming. Knew she could pull away. Told herself that was just what she should do. Irrationally, illogically, she leaned right into the kiss. She went up on her toes to meet his mouth with hers. Her body molded to his. Her arms came up to lock around his neck. In the process, the still spouting garden hose sprayed the assembled crowd indiscriminately, producing yelps from the customers and a startled squawk from Hank.

Sabrina hardly heard their shouts. Barely noticed when her disgusted boss yanked the hose out of her hand.

"Give me that," he muttered. "Those two fools need a dunkin' more'n we do."

She relinquished the hose without a murmur. Wet and on fire at the same time, she lost herself in Jack's kiss. Her knees turned to dishwater. Her hips canted into his. Her heart pounded, and the low-angled sun blazed on her closed eyelids. By the time Jack raised his head, she'd forgotten how to breathe.

"I'll be back," he whispered hoarsely. "Later."

"I get off early tonight," she answered, her voice as low and ragged as his.

"How early?"

"Nine."

He stared down at her a moment longer. Sabrina could see the silver flecks in his blue eyes. Detect the promise in his slow, toe-curling grin.

"Nine. Right."

"Make it nine-thirty. My place."

Still breathless, she murmured her address in Dunford, where she'd rented a tiny, boxlike house from one of Peg's cousins. The sleepy little town was only a few miles from the diner.

It was only after Jack had herded Al to the red pickup that Sabrina came hurtling back to earth. All it took to bring her down was one glimpse of the Wentworth Oil Works logo on the door panel. She landed with a thump as Jack drove off.

Smart, she told herself in gathering dismay and self-disgust. Real smart. Fall right into the man's arms, why don't you? Billionaire Joseph Wentworth's grandson decides to go slumming for a few hours, and the ditzy waitress drapes herself all over him.

She could just imagine what Jack Wentworth thought he was coming back to at nine-thirty tonight!

Sucking on the split knuckle of his right hand, Jack gripped the steering wheel with his left. His blood still pounded from the brawl...and from that astonishing kiss. He couldn't wait to dump Ali at the airport, get himself cleaned up, and retrace his tracks to Dunford…and Sabrina.

He wheeled onto I-44 and let the accelerator inch up to the speed limit. Hot concrete whirred under the truck's tires. A mix of gentle hills, green pastures and woodland went past in a blur. Fat rolls of new-cut hay shimmered red gold in the rays of the slowly descending sun, and the scent of fresh-mown Bermuda grass blew in through the open windows.

The exit for Glenpool sped by, then the off-ramp for Sapulpa. A few minutes later, Tulsa's distinctive skyline loomed in the distance. The tall skyscrapers gleamed a liquid gold in the reflection of the low-hanging sun. Without the least difficulty, Jack picked out Wentworth Oil's corporate headquarters, a slash of granite and glass cutting into the hazy blue sky. His grandfather had laid the cornerstone for that building, as he was so fond of reminding Jack and his younger sister and brother. The old man damn well expected his grandchildren to live up to his name and his building.

Every day for almost forty years Joseph had driven from the sprawling stone mansion he'd built in the Oklahoma hills halfway between Stillwater and Tulsa to oversee his growing financial empire. Even after Jack took over the corporate reins, the eighteenth floor presidential suite remained Joseph's and Joseph's alone. His stroke had slowed him down some, but he was still enough of a crusty old bastard that men like that drunk back at the diner would recall him after just one meeting.

Although…

Jack's brow creased in a frown. Now that his blood had cooled, the whole encounter outside the diner began to strike him as a little off.

"Do you remember what the mean one…Sam… said?" he asked Ali slowly. "About seeing me and my grandfather in Ardmore?"

The prince cocked his head. Stroking his mustache, he thought back. "He said he saw you and Joseph a few years ago in this place you speak of, when someone took pictures."

Jack's fist tightened on the steering wheel. "That photo shoot for *Life* took place almost a decade ago, and now that I think about it, it didn't take place in Ardmore."

"Perhaps this so ugly one confused the place and the time."

"Perhaps. He sure didn't have any trouble placing me, though. Or you."

Across the leather seat, his gaze caught Ali's. He knew without asking that the prince was now running the same set of questions through his mind.

Why would the man lie about seeing him and his grandfather? If he had, how did he really know Jack's identity? And how had the little runt picked up that Ali was from the Middle East? The prince had an accent, sure, but not one that most people would immediately place. In his jeans and borrowed Stetson, he could have easily been taken for a Hispanic American, or a Latino.

What was more, Jack thought grimly, the two combatants had wielded their fists with a whole lot more accuracy than their inebriated status should have allowed. Doubt hardening into suspicion, he snatched up his mobile phone. One press of a button patched him through to his office. A moment later, his efficient assistant forwarded his call to the Route 66 Diner.

"Yeah?"

He couldn't mistake Hank's grumble. "This is Jack Wentworth. Are those two drunks still there?"

"Nah. They slunk off right after you left. I don't 'spect they'll be back this way anytime soon."

"Right. Thanks."

Still frowning, Jack flipped the phone shut. He should have gotten their license number. Nailed down their names and the reason behind their belligerence. Some undercover operative he was!

Trey McGill echoed that sentiment a few moments later. He was pacing the ramp when Jack brought the pickup to a squealing stop beside a sleek, two-engine jet parked on a controlled access apron at the Tulsa International Airport. The white-and-black flag of Qatar gleamed on the jet's tail. A glimpse through the open hatch and lowered stairs showed the gleam of polished teak and deep, plush carpets.

Trey took one look at Jack's face and Ali's bloodied shirt, and his careful State Department demeanor came apart at the seams. "What the hell happened to you two?"

"I'll tell you later," Jack said grimly. "Let's get the prince in the air first."

Brushing past the gray-suited bureaucrat, he accompanied Ali to the jet's staircase. Trey followed, his face tight with anxiety.

"Dammit, Wentworth, what's going on?"

Ignoring him, Jack gripped Ali's hand. "Better get moving. I don't know who those characters were, but I'll find out, I promise you."

"What characters?" McGill demanded.

"Have a safe journey home, my friend."

Ali clapped his free hand on Jack's forearm. His fingers dug deep. "May Allah watch over you until we meet again."

"And you."

Halfway up the jet's stairs, the prince turned to give Jack a thumbs-up. "It was a good fight, was it not? And unless I mistake the matter, you have won a most precious prize."

The moment Ali stepped inside, the stairs whirred up and into the compartment below the hatchway. The door slammed shut.

"What fight?" McGill thrust a hand through his short, sandy hair. "What prize?"

At the low, warning whir of the jet's twin engines, Jack pulled the State Department rep back to a safe distance. The cadre of plainclothes security men Trey had posted around the plane retreated as well.

The whir rose to a shrill whine, then a deafening roar. A cloud of engine exhaust and fuel-scented heat enveloped the small group of watchers. The jet rolled down the taxiway, looking like a small, sharp bird of prey amid the larger passenger jets.

Trey's handheld radio stuttered. His mouth still tight, he lifted it and issued the necessary instructions to give the private jet priority for takeoff. Moments later, the aircraft lifted into the sky and banked to the east with the soaring grace of a gull. McGill waited only until the noise died enough for him to be heard. Planting himself squarely before Jack, he demanded an explanation.

"Okay, Wentworth, what's going on."

"I'm not sure," Jack replied grimly.

Paring the extended stop at the diner down to its bare essentials, he briefed Trey on the near accident and brawl with the two supposed drunks.

McGill's gray eyes narrowed on Jack's face. "But you don't think it was an accident?"

"Looking back, I can see that the whole incident was too damned pat." He rubbed a hand across his neck. "The truck peeled off the road and into the parking lot the exact moment Ali and I stepped out of the diner. It was almost as if they were waiting for us."

"Dammit!" Trey slapped the radio against the palm of his other hand. "I knew I shouldn't have let you and the prince go wandering off through the countryside like that!"

Jack didn't comment on that. Both he and McGill knew that there was no "let" about it. Jack was a private citizen. He performed secret, often dangerous missions for his country out of a sense of patriotism…and a restlessness his corporate responsibilities couldn't quite satisfy. Although he and Trey had

worked together for years now, the government bureaucrat didn't have the authority to dictate the oil
executive's movements. Trey's responsibility was to
support them.

Tight-jawed, Trey dug a leather-bound notebook
and gold ballpoint pen out of his suit pocket. "Give
me what details you can on those two hoods. I'll run
them by the FBI and CIA."

Succinctly, Jack described the tall, thin Sam and
shorter Digger. Trey's pen scribbled furiously.

"What about their vehicle?"

"A black Ford pickup, '88 or '89, with a dented
right rear fender and two long scrapes along the truck
bed. It carried Oklahoma plates, but I didn't get the
number."

That was the last time he'd make that mistake, Jack
vowed silently.

"And the others at this diner?"

He shot McGill a quick look.

"Someone had to have coordinated the attack," the
State Department rep said grimly. "Maybe that someone followed you into the restaurant and handed you
off to the two outside when you stepped out the
door."

Frowning, Jack ran the other occupants of the diner
through his mind. "I don't think so. I don't remember
seeing anyone act in a suspicious manner."

Trey tapped his notebook with his pen, his eyes
hard. "Yeah, well, you didn't suspect Sam and his
buddy of anything more than drunken belligerence at
first, either."

"Not at first," he conceded, rubbing a palm across his sore knuckles.

The gold pen tapped on the notebook. "Who else was at the diner? I'll check them out."

"Three truckers," Jack replied slowly. "One of whom was driving a TransAmerica eighteen-wheeler with Texas plates and a green-and-silver cab. Two men who looked like locals. The owner, a former sailor called Hank Donovan. And the waitresses, a Peg Something and a Sabrina Jensen."

"Any one of them could have been in on it," Trey muttered.

"Not Sabrina Jensen. She saved my butt with a water hose."

McGill's gaze locked with his. "You've been in this business almost as long as I have, Wentworth. What better way to gain someone's trust than to do them a favor? Or appear to do them one?"

Jack bit back an instinctive protest. He would have bet everything he had that Sabrina was exactly what she appeared to be, an intelligent, hardworking, damnably seductive brunette with a mouth he would dream about for a long time to come. But he'd already made one mistake today by taking those two cowboys for mere drunks. He'd let Trey run his checks. In the meantime, he'd do a little checking of his own.

His face tight, McGill flipped his notebook shut. "That's not much to go on, but I'll see what I can do. Maybe the system will have something on them."

"Maybe." Flexing his shoulders to ease the ache from one of Sam's flying punches, Jack strode toward his truck. "I'm stopping at my place in Tulsa to clean up, then I'll head back to talk to Ms. Jensen."

Frowning, Trey followed on his heels. "Why?"

"It bothers me that I miscued those two characters. I want to make sure I didn't miss anything else."

"I don't think that's a good idea."

"You run your system checks, Trey. I've got a more personal one-on-one in mind."

McGill's gray eyes narrowed on Jack's face. "There's more to this situation than what you've told me, isn't there?"

"No. But there could be," he added under his breath, keying the ignition. "If I get lucky."

Trey slapped a hand on the open window frame. "It's the woman, isn't it?"

"Maybe."

Disgust rippled across his patrician features. "It's always a woman with you, Wentworth."

Jack could have told him that this one was different. That he sensed a strength and a ready laughter in Sabrina that Heather had never shown during their brief, tragic acquaintance. That the waitress had triggered something deep inside him from the first moment he'd seen her with her feet propped up and her face turned to the sun.

Trey didn't need to hear that. Not from him. Not at this point, anyway. Instead, Jack simply nodded a goodbye and put the pickup into drive.

Chapter 4

Trey McGill could access government sources. The CEO of Wentworth Oil Works could access a few of his own.

With his eyes on the light traffic left over from Tulsa's evening rush, Jack snatched up his mobile phone and punched the direct line to his office. Although it was now well past seven, he didn't have any doubt that his executive assistant would still be at work. Pete Hastings lived and breathed Wentworth Oil. He had since he'd tried to wheedle twenty bucks off Jack six years ago. Jack had hired him on the spot, seeing through the panhandler's outer scruffiness to the con artist underneath. No one, but no one, got past Pete unless they carried Jack's personal stamp of approval.

Sure enough, his assistant answered the phone on the first ring.

"I need you to run a background check for me on a Sabrina Jensen," Jack said without preamble.

"The usual stuff? Credit check, employment history, driving record?"

"Right."

Gut instinct told Jack the check wouldn't turn up anything, but he wasn't taking any more chances. Besides, he was curious about her. More than curious.

"I'll get on it right away."

"Call me back as soon as you can. I'll be at the apartment for the next hour or so."

"Will do."

The sun had slipped behind the downtown skyscrapers, leaving the city to bask in a hazy summer twilight by the time Jack turned onto the ramp for the underground garage of The Towers on Riverside Drive. He kept an apartment at the high-rise for those late nights when he didn't want to drive to the sprawling Wentworth estate on the other side of Tulsa.

The red pickup rolled to a stop beside his midnight blue Jag. Jack preferred a company vehicle most of the time, particularly on his frequent visits to production sites around the state. Some of the roads hadn't improved all that much from the early days of the great wildcat strikes. The Jaguar served for those occasions when he had to deal with men impressed by the trappings that came with his position and his background.

Keying in a code for the private elevator, he used

the short ride to tug off his ball cap and whack it
against his pant leg. Clouds of red Oklahoma dust
swirled around the elevator and settled on the expensive brass fixtures. Moments later, the elevator
whirred to a halt at the penthouse level. The doors
slid open, and Jack walked into the large, airy apartment he shared with the feisty older woman who
styled herself his housekeeper and self-appointed spir-
itual advisor.

Strolling through the foyer, he hooked his cap on
the stag antlers that framed a massive mirror. His
boots echoed on the polished oak flooring that gave
onto the plush, gray-carpeted living room. Directly
ahead, a floor-to-ceiling glass wall afforded an eye-
popping view. The Arkansas River meandered south
like a wide, silver ribbon cutting through the twilight.
Lights from the exclusive homes all along the river
twinkled like early stars.

The living room was sparsely furnished in hand-
wrought native oak pieces and decorated with only a
few of the Frederic Remington bronzes the Wentworths had collected over the years. It had an un-
cluttered air that suited Jack perfectly and made it
easy for Hannah to keep dust-free and shiny. A rattle
of pans in the kitchen pinpointed her location.

"Hey, Hannah."

A pixie face framed by a riot of carroty orange
curls that defiantly belied her sixty-plus years poked
through the kitchen door.

"Jack? You're home earlier than—" She broke
off, her raisin black eyes rounding as she took in his

bloodied shirt. "Who'd you get crosswise with, boy?"

"A couple of guys who took exception to my pretty face," he returned dryly.

"Pretty?" She hooted. "What were they, blind drunk?"

"To all appearances."

The swinging kitchen door whooshed behind her. Crossing to his side, she squinted up at the cut above his eye. Jack had been trying to convince her to wear glasses for years with minimal results.

"I better put some antiseptic on that cut."

"I'll take care of it."

"You and your granddaddy are two of a kind," she scolded, shaking her orangey red curls. "Neither one of you could ever stand any fussing."

Since Hannah and Joseph Wentworth had shared one blazing summer of passion five or six years ago, Jack figured she knew what she was talking about. After Hannah and Old Joe parted company, she'd taken up residence with Jack.

The arrangement worked wonderfully. Jack was gone more than he was home, and Hannah had plenty of room to host her frequent gatherings. So far, thank goodness, none of the palmists or tarot card readers she invited in had stumbled upon Jack's double life. Hannah wouldn't have approved...any more than she approved of the fact that he was still unmarried at thirty-five.

She did approve of the fact that he was going right

out again, though. She positively beamed when he
told her he'd just come home to change.

"Good! My Second Life group is meeting here tonight. We can meditate better without you clumping
through the place."

Humming, she palmed the kitchen door and returned to her pots and pans. Jack sniffed the air as he
made his way to the master bath. Apparently the med-
itators were getting one of Hannah's eighty-proof
chocolate rum cakes. With luck, he might be able to
wheedle a piece for himself before he left.

The return call from Peter came just as he was tow-
eling himself off after a quick, steaming shower.
Slinging the towel around his neck, he took the call
on the extension in the man-size bathroom.

"I don't know what you were looking for, boss,
but this Sabrina Jensen is clean, squeaky clean."

"I wasn't looking for anything in particular. Just
give me the details."

"Born, Amarillo, Texas. Moved to Oklahoma at
age thirteen. Current age, twenty-four. Five foot six.
Brown hair. Green eyes. One hundred nineteen and a
half pounds according to her last driver's license."

Jack smiled at the mist-covered mirror. Wherever
Sabrina packed that half pound, it looked good on her.
Damn good.

"I got one of our friends at the police department
to check their computers. She has no traffic history,
no prior arrests, no outstanding warrants, not even a
citation for jaywalking."

"What about family?"

"Her student loan application at OSU shows she has a twin sister living in Oklahoma City and a father who owns his own rig and pulls cross-country hauls. Evidently she doesn't receive any income from either of them. She's worked a list of part-time jobs two pages long since she turned fifteen. Most of her income these days goes for rent and for her tuition and books at Oklahoma State."

Everything fit with the impression Jack had formed of Sabrina Jensen and with the information he'd already obtained at the diner. The woman certainly wasn't afraid of hard work.

"Her credit rating looked good at first pass," his assistant continued, "but I'll do some more digging tomorrow when I can get into the financial databases."

"Thanks, Pete. You've done good. As usual."

"Remember that when I talk to you about my next raise."

"As if you'd let me forget," Jack returned, smiling.

He hung up a few moments later, thinking through the information Pete had fed him. Unless Trey turned up something startling through his own sources, he was satisfied. More than satisfied.

He was also, he discovered, impatient as hell to see Sabrina again. Just thinking of the way her mouth had fit under his pushed him to a state of near arousal. The memory of her body pressed against his brought him even closer to the edge.

Shoving his shirttails into the waistband of a clean pair of jeans, he rolled the sleeves, then snatched up his wallet and keys. A moment later, he settled a summer straw Resistol on his still damp hair and left with a shouted goodbye to Hannah. Opting for the company truck again instead of the flashy Jag, Jack wheeled out of the garage into a soft, purple night.

By the time he pulled into the driveway of a modest bungalow in Dunford, his state of semiarousal had edged dangerously close to rock hardness. He couldn't believe that he felt so much like a pimply-faced teenager on his first date...until he remembered Sabrina's breathlessness when they broke off that shattering kiss this afternoon. Anticipation zinged through Jack's veins. He checked his watch.

Nine-twenty-two.

Close enough.

He cut across the tiny yard toward the front door, his step eager. He didn't exactly have deliberate seduction in mind, but he certainly had high expectations of taking another taste of that soft, full mouth home with him tonight. Or tomorrow. Or whenever Sabrina decided to send him on his way.

What he didn't expect was the distinct lack of welcome in her face when she opened the door.

"Hello, Sabrina."

"Jack."

In one swift glance, he took in every detail of her appearance. She'd released her hair from its loose knot. The mink dark mass fell in silky waves to her collarbone. She'd exchanged the white knit top for a tunic in a bright cherry red that made her skin look creamy and so soft that Jack's fingers itched to stroke it. She'd even traded her jeans and sneakers for skirty little canvas shorts and sandals.

He might have taken that long length of bare leg as a signal of great things to come if not for Sabrina's closed, unsmiling face. She didn't invite him in. She didn't release her grip on the doorknob.

Pulling off his straw Resistol, he smiled down at her. "Am I too early? Or too late?"

Okay, Sabrina told herself. All right. She could do this. Ignoring the sudden pinging in her rib cage directly attributable to Jack's crooked smile, she took a steadying breath.

"I tried to call you," she told him with a touch of coolness. "Your home phone is unlisted, and the folks on the Wentworth Oil switchboard said they weren't authorized to give out the number."

He cocked his head, clearly surprised at her tone. The light from the porch lamps picked up the damp gleam in his short, dark hair. He'd showered, Sabrina saw, and slapped on an expensive aftershave. She'd sniffed that rich, tangy scent before—at one of Tulsa's most expensive department stores.

Perversely, the idea that Jack had gussied up for her stiffened Sabrina's resolve to send him right back to his truck. She'd had plenty of time to regret her uninhibited response to his kiss. Just because the Wentworths owned half of Oklahoma and she slung chicken-fried steak for a living didn't mean he could play games with her. Loan or no loan, kiss or no kiss,

her prickly pride stung her every time she remembered how he'd let her think he was some down-and-
out rigger…and how *she'd* let him sweep her into his
arms after she'd learned his real identity. She could
just imagine what spin he'd put on that.

"Sorry," he said in answer to her stiff little speech.
"I'll give you a number where I can be contacted,
night or day."

"That won't be necessary."

He couldn't mistake her message this time. His
brow arched, but he gave it one more shot.

"It may not be necessary, but I'm hoping you'll
use the number, Sabrina, whenever you want."

"I don't think so."

"Did I miss something this afternoon? I thought
you invited me out here tonight?"

"I did." Impatiently, she hooked her hair behind
her left ear. "Look, I'm sorry you drove all the way
out here, but it's late and…"

"And?"

She pulled in another deep breath. She might as
well get the matter out in the open.

"And I'm too tired to indulge you in any more
slumming."

"What?"

"I must have given you both a real chuckle," she
said, shaking her head in disgust. "I practically fell
all over you this afternoon. Trust me, I don't make a
practice of that kind of behavior."

"I didn't think you did."

Her chin lifted. "Particularly not with oil baron's

grandsons and playboy princes who get their kicks by passing themselves off as down-at-the-heel riggers.''

Jack went still. The sudden, swift look he gave her from narrowed eyes told Sabrina it was time to end this farce.

''Now if you'll excuse me, I have an accounting test to study for.''

She shut the door in his face.

Or tried to.

The man who quietly but forcefully caught the door's edge sent a ripple of unease down her spine. He wasn't the same blue-eyed charmer who'd teased her out of her sleepy doze earlier this afternoon. Certainly not the laughing rigger who'd swept her into his arms.

She held her ground, but it took some doing. His eyes lasered into hers with an intensity that raised the hairs on the back of her neck.

''Just to set the record straight,'' he said slowly, ''you're the one who assumed we were riggers.''

She conceded the point with something less than grace. ''You're right. I'll think twice before I associate someone in a Wentworth truck and ball cap with a shrieking oil pump in the future!''

Ignoring her biting sarcasm, he held her eyes with his own. ''I don't remember either Al or I mentioning that he was a prince.''

''Oh, really?'' Her hands went to her hips. ''As I recall, he offered to whisk me away to Qatar in his private jet and drape me in emeralds and pearls. If he doesn't want people to assume he's a prince or a sultan or something, he needs to come up with another approach.''

Jack stared down at her, his mind racing. Trey's suspicions had come rushing back with a vengeance. Neither the U.S. nor Qatar had leaked the prince's short, unscheduled visit to the press or the public. The endowment of the petroleum research facility at OSU—the ostensible reason for his visit—wouldn't be announced until later this month. By then, the secret accord Ali was carrying back to his country would have been acted upon by the Gulf Cooperation Council. It was to maintain that low profile that Jack had suggested they both don comfortable jeans and work shirts for the impromptu detour through Oklahoma's back roads en route to the airport.

Even at the Route 66 Diner, they'd been careful to give no hints as to Ali's royal status. Despite his extravagant gallantry and outrageous offers to Sabrina, Ali had never said his full name or his rank. Evidently, he hadn't needed to. She'd reached her own conclusions.

Looking down into her indignant green eyes, Jack couldn't bring himself to believe it was anything other than a guess. Nor did he believe she'd had anything to do with the attack by Sam and his buddy, Digger. Relaxing muscles that had gone taut and still, he shoved a hand through his hair. It was time to mend a few bridges.

''I guess I need to come up with another approach, too. I'm sorry I misled you, Sabrina. Do you want the truth?''

"That would be a nice change," she tossed back.

"I let you think I'd lost my wallet because it was a handy excuse to come back and see you tonight." A rueful smile tugged at his mouth. "I still owe you for the hamburger and Al's pie, remember?"

Instead of softening her tight, wary expression, his confession seemed to stiffen her up even more.

"I told you it was on the house."

"I always pay for what I want."

"Is that right?" Her head went back. Green sparks flashed in her eyes. "I hope you're not expecting anything more for your money than an onion burger and some pie, Wentworth."

"Whoa! You don't believe in stepping lightly over rough ground, do you?"

"No, I don't. Nor do I believe in deliberately misleading people."

"I'll keep that in mind."

"You do that," she muttered, less belligerent now, but still stiff.

Jack hadn't moved in diplomatic circles for years without learning when to advance and when to retreat. This particular situation called for a little bit of both.

"Why don't we start over?" He held out his hand. "I'm Jack Wentworth, onetime tool pusher and now full-time paper pusher."

She hesitated so long he'd begun to think she wouldn't settle for anything less than a full retreat. Reluctantly, she put her hand in his.

"Sabrina Jensen, part-time student, full-time waitress, and all-time history buff."

Releasing her hand, Jack smiled. "Hank told me you were responsible for restoring the diner. You've done a heck of a job."

"Thanks." For the first time since she opened the door, a hint of animation came into her face. "My dad's a truck driver. He used to take my sister and me along on his runs when we were little. I guess I grew up eating road dust and washing it down with stories of Route 66 in its days of glory."

Inspiration struck. Without a qualm, Jack jettisoned his plans to accompany his sister to the opera tomorrow night.

The Wentworths made a point of supporting local artists by attending every performance, but Josie could darn well rope their younger brother, Michael, into duty for tomorrow's gala. Spoiled, completely uninterested in the oil business, and far too often at odds with his irascible grandfather, Michael needed something to keep him out of trouble.

"Look, Sabrina, I'm not slumming. Nor am I looking for anything more than a few hours spent in the company of an intriguing woman."

She was still digesting that when he played his ace.

"It would be my honor, ma'am, if you'd let me escort you to the Sapulpa Route 66 Blowout and Art Show tomorrow night. I've been told it's the best gathering of vintage cars and road buffs in the state."

"It is," she agreed, torn between exasperation and amusement at the man's persistence. "I've gone for the past two years in a row."

She'd also asked for time off to go tomorrow night,

too. Sabrina fully intended to lose herself in the lively, lighthearted festivities. She just hadn't intended to lose herself with Jack Wentworth. The idea sent a spear of pleasure through her...until her stubborn, hardheaded pride kicked in again.

In retrospect, she shouldn't have been the least surprised that Jack had zeroed in on her passion for the historic highway. From what she'd heard and read about the Wentworths, the family always got what they went after, whether it was another line of tankers to add to their fleet, or a waitress for a quick tumble on a hot summer night.

A refusal had already formed on her lips when Jack settled the straw hat on his head once more and reached for the doorknob.

"What time do you want me to pick you up tomorrow?"

Sabrina blinked. He was leaving? Just like that? After all the nasty motives she'd ascribed to his little subterfuge? After berating herself all afternoon for going hollow-heeled over his kiss? She'd expected him to pounce tonight, or at least try to pick up where they left off earlier this afternoon. His good-natured retreat disarmed her totally.

"Well..."

With an easy coordination of muscle and grace, he reached into his back pocket and pulled out his wallet. Sabrina stiffened, but he didn't make the mistake of insisting on paying for his meal again. Instead, he dug out a small card and handed it to her.

"Here. This is my private number. It'll catch me

at home or on the move. Call me and let me know what you decide.''

Sabrina's thumb moved over the embossed lettering. Despite the stern talking-to she'd given herself about idiotic waitresses who let themselves get carried away by a grin and lazy blue eyes, her throat tightened as she watched Jack stride away. His long legs ate up her minuscule front lawn.

Damn! These Oklahoma boys did things to a pair of jeans that no one east of the Mississippi could begin to imagine.

She bit her lip. She should just let him go! She didn't have time for fun and games with someone who'd shown himself a master at them. The man was completely out of her league.

The arguments rolled around for all of five or six seconds. The darkness had almost swallowed him when she heard herself call out.

"Jack!"

He turned, his face shadowed under the brim of his hat.

"I'm off tomorrow night. Pick me up at six."

Chapter 5

Friday dished up the kind of glorious summer night that women dream about and men take for granted.

Sabrina had slipped away from work at four, leaving Peg and a high school part-timer to handle the evening crowd. Thankfully, she didn't have to rely on the air-conditioning in the used Mazda she'd bought five years ago to cool her down on the way home. The soul-sucking heat of July and dog days of August were some weeks off. The early June's sun still felt like warm silk on her skin.

A long, sybaritic soak in a tub full of bubbles and a splash of body freshener added their own special tingle. She took her time blow-drying her hair, using a round styling brush to tame the thick mane. When she was finished, the dark brown mass fell in a

smooth sweep to her shoulders, curling just a bit upward at the ends. A touch of dusky shadow brought
out the seaweed green of her eyes. Lip liner and a
few strokes of blush added a touch of pink to her sun-
browned skin.

She debated for less than thirty seconds over what
to wear. After spending most of her day in jeans and
sneakers, she wanted cool and comfortable. A little
sexy wouldn't hurt, either. That left her with only one
choice…the halter-necked sundress in bright, lemony
yellow that her more flamboyant twin, Rachel, had
insisted she purchase during a long-ago shopping expedition.

The bare-backed dress certainly qualified as cool
and comfortable. The jersey fabric also happened to
cling in just the right places. Despite its almost ankle-
length skirt and demure, crossover neckline, the silky
stretch of yellow left zero tolerance for extra pounds.
If nothing else, Sabrina thought with a wry glance at
the mirror, the frantic pace at the diner kept her trim
enough to wear the thing.

A pair of low-heeled white sandals and a funky
charm bracelet made of old soda bottle caps and plastic sunflowers completed her ensemble. She was just
slipping on the bracelet when she heard the rumble
of a noisy muffler pulling into her drive. She threw a
quick look at the clock beside her bed.

Five-forty-seven. Jack was early…again. She'd
have to remember that particular character trait in the
future. Spritzing on a few sprays of perfume, she

snatched up her purse and left the bedroom on a cloud of woodsy rose scent and anticipation.

The realization that she was already thinking in terms of a future caught her halfway to the front door. Deliberately, she slowed her eager step. She'd better get a grip here. And she'd better remember what happened when her mother had let her hormones get the best of her common sense. After abandoning Sabrina's dad and the twins, Blanche had jettisoned her handsome rodeo cowboy not long afterward. Or maybe he'd jettisoned her. The last Sabrina had heard, her mother was currently on husband number four or five. She'd stopped sending even sporadic birthday cards years ago, and her daughters had stopped counting her husbands.

That sobering reminder put a lid on Sabrina's bubbling anticipation and steadied her skittery pulse... until she opened the front door.

"Oh, my."

As greetings went, that one was about as inane as any she'd ever uttered. At that moment, however, she couldn't think of anything more sophisticated.

How in the world could Jack Wentworth turn a crisp white cotton shirt, well-washed jeans, and a pair of low-heeled boots into a portrait of sheer masculinity that any female between the ages of nine and ninety would pant over? Maybe it was the strong, tanned forearms revealed by the rolled-back sleeves. Or the way his jeans fit snug around his lean hips, needing no belt to hold them up. Or that damned

smile that started at his mouth, spread to eyes shaded
by his straw Resistol, and left Sabrina almost melting
in a puddle of yellow jersey.

"Ditto that," he said, his admiring gaze never leaving her face.

Pleasure pinpricked through her veins, following
hard on the heels of that first, instinctive admiration.
Common sense finally came in a distant third.

For heaven's sake! She was practically drooling
over the man! She'd better remember who he was.
His shirt might not sport a trendy designer logo on
the pocket, but she'd bet one of Tulsa's most exclusive tailors had hand-fit it across those broad shoulders. And she knew darn well his tooled leather Justin
boots cost more than she made in a month. The grandson of an oil baron might spend an evening at a street
fair in Sapulpa with a waitress, but he'd look to the
current crop of debutantes when he decided to get
serious.

Which was fine with her, she reaffirmed as she
locked the front door behind her. That was all she
was looking for, too…a pleasant evening at a street
fair with an attractive man.

Her first inkling of what was to come occurred
when she caught sight of the shining, cream-colored
convertible parked in her driveway. Its curved fend-
ers, itty-bitty round taillights, several tons of chrome,
and six-inch white-walls harked back to an era of bygone splendor.

"What *is* that?" she gasped.

"A '53 Corvette." Grinning at her open-mouthed awe, Jack escorted her to the gleaming two-seater. "I borrowed it from a friend. He usually participates in the Poker Run at the Blowout."

The Poker Run, Sabrina knew, was a competitive event with rules that only the classic car buffs who drove it seemed to understand. She couldn't believe anyone would pass up the chance to enter this beauty in the fun until Jack explained.

"Dennis's wife is in labor with their second child. From what I gathered, it was a close call, but he opted to stay with Lisa for the birth. There were tears in his eyes when he handed me the keys to the 'Vette, though."

"Poor baby."

"That's what I said."

"I wasn't referring to your friend."

He opened the passenger door, his blue eyes dancing. "Neither was I."

Laughing, Sabrina settled into a cloud-soft seat that smelled of leather polish and endless hours of loving care. Her fascinated gaze took in the mammoth, chrome-decorated steering wheel and minuscule round indicator dials on the dash.

"This car must have been *made* for roads like the old Route 66," she breathed.

"It was." A twist of the ignition produced the kind of full-barreled rumble rarely heard from today's quieter engines. "You're sitting in America's first pro-

duction sports car. This baby—or ones like her—
cruised the highways all across the country.''

"Can you imagine all the drive-up hamburger
stands and movie theaters she must have pulled
into?''

Sighing, Sabrina buckled the seat belt obviously
installed post production. The car stirred her imagination, already well-tuned to the era she was trying
to re-create at the diner. During their childhood, she
and Rachel had spent a lot of time on the roads with
their father. Their unconventional upbringing had
spawned in her a stubborn independence, a fierce loy-
alty to her itinerant father and flighty twin…and an
appreciation of the rich history of America's highways.

That history came alive for her when they drove
down Sapulpa's Main Street a half hour later. Once
part of the Mother Road that stretched unbroken from
Chicago to California, the tree-shaded street was lined
with restored buildings that marked the town's tran-
sition from an 1880s cattle and agricultural railhead
to a turn-of-the-century oil boomtown. Sapulpa's
Main Street now served as the focus for the annual
conclave of Route 66 nuts, and they had certainly
come out in full force tonight!

Vintage cars, trucks and motorcycles filled every
available parking space, drawing throngs of admirers.
Sabrina caught flashes of sky blue Bel-Aires, fin-
tailed pink Cadillacs, mammoth green Hudsons, and
even a chrome-laden Edsel. Local artists and crafters

had set up displays along the sidewalks. Merchants hawked T-shirts, posters and ball caps to the tourists. Antique shops displayed Mother Road memorabilia in every window. Over the noise of the crowd, a dee-jay spun period music. As Jack made the turn into a parking lot just off Main, a version of Bobby Troup's 1946 classic, "Get Your Kicks on Route 66," eddied over the airwaves.

But it was the food vendors who were doing the busiest business at this hour. Even they had gotten into the spirit, dishing up authentic foods and specials from the golden days of the Mother Road. Hamburgers sizzled. Frankfurters steamed. Fried chicken and chicken-fried steak were stacked high on paper platters. A vintage, bicycle-powered ice-cream cart catered to an eager crowd of youngsters and oldsters alike.

"I wish I could talk Hank into setting up a booth at the Blowout," Sabrina murmured. "His onion burgers would have everyone here making tracks back to our diner."

Jack smiled as he eased the Corvette into a tight parking space. He knew darn well what had pulled him back to the diner, and it wasn't Hank's onion burgers. If he'd needed any proof, he got it when he walked around the low-slung convertible to help Sabrina out. Her bracelet jangled as she put her hand in his, and her smile heated him up inside like a section of steel pipe left lying too long in the sun. That silky slide of brilliant yellow that covered her front and bared her back didn't exactly help matters, either.

His stomach coiling with a combination of pleasure and anticipation, he tucked her hand in the crook of his arm. They'd only taken a step or two when she dug her nails into his sleeve.

"Listen!"

With some effort, Jack tried to sort through the varying levels of noise. He heard kids shouting. A car honking. Two Harley-Davidsons revving in the distance. But nothing that would put such a reverent shine in Sabrina's eyes.

"That's Woody Guthrie," she said excitedly. "It must be from a rerecording of the *Dust Bowl Ballads.*"

Jack cocked his head, listening to the plaintive lyrics pouring from loudspeakers like crackling wine. With simple eloquence, the dry-voiced folk singer told of the birth and death of so many Okies' dreams as they took the road west to escape the bank failures and relentless droughts of the thirties.

"He did twelve records in that series," Sabrina mused as they joined the crowds on Main Street. "They're so sad, and so uplifting."

Jack had only a hazy knowledge of the Oklahoma folk poet who became a model for later folk singers like Bob Dylan and Tom Paxton. Sabrina, however, seemed to have absorbed his history along with that of the famous highway he once traveled.

"I think I read somewhere that he wrote or recorded more than a thousand songs,'' she said at the conclusion of the ballad.

''Including 'This Land Is Your Land,' if I remember correctly.''

She nodded. ''That's one of his most famous, but I have to admit the *Dust Bowl Ballads* are my favorites. They really capture the pathos of the times…and the immense dignity of the human spirit.''

Jack was impressed. Born and bred in Oklahoma, he'd grown up with a native's casual acceptance of its rich history. He had an insider's appreciation of the rough-and-tumble oil business, of course, and kept a close watch on his grandfather's varied cattle and agricultural interests throughout the state. More directly, he saw to it that Wentworth Oil made hefty donations each year to various enterprises to preserve Oklahoma history, like tonight's Blowout.

He didn't devote the passion to it, though, that Sabrina apparently did. As she described the various recordings Woody Guthrie had made to protest unemployment and social injustice, a vibrant, fascinating woman emerged. A woman far more complex than her background and present occupation would suggest to the casual observer.

And Jack would hardly qualify as casual. He wasn't quite sure when he'd passed that stage. Yesterday afternoon when he'd covered her mouth with his, probably. If not then, last night, for sure. He hadn't particularly relished turning away from Sabrina's front door less than two minutes after approaching. After the fever of anticipation he'd experienced during the drive to her place, her accusation that he'd come slumming took some swallowing. He'd gotten it down, though. So had she, if the eager look on her face was any indication.

More intrigued than ever by the luscious, contradictory brunette at his side, he slipped a hand under her elbow to steer her through the boisterous crowd. Slowly, they worked their way down Main. Shops crammed with relics of the Mother Road drew oohs and sighs from Sabrina, but Jack's attention stayed riveted on the woman at his side. Her skin felt silky soft under his fingers, and the seductive swirl of her dress about her hips had him—

"Jack!" The boom of a hearty female voice jerked his head up. "Jack Wentworth!"

"Hello, Mayor Boyd."

Like a majestic ocean liner cutting the waves, Mildred Boyd sailed through the crowd. Half a head taller than those around her, she wore cherry red leather boots and a red straw Stetson sporting Route 66 buttons in every color of the rainbow.

She greeted Jack with a thump between the shoulder blades that rattled his back teeth. "I didn't know you were coming to the Blowout."

"I didn't either, until last night."

Surreptitiously rolling his shoulders, he introduced Sabrina to one of Oklahoma's most colorful and far-sighted city leaders.

"Sabrina's a real aficionado of America's Main

Street, too," he added. "She's helping restore the Route 66 Diner outside Dunford."

"So you're the brains behind that project!" The mayor's mega-decibel voice had heads turning up and down the street. "Couldn't believe the place last time I stopped in. We'll have to get you involved in the 66 Preservation Society, girl. In fact, I could use some help with the four-state rally we're planning for next spring."

Sabrina tried to plead work and school, but the mayor steamrollered right over her halfhearted objections.

"Anyone who can get Hank off his butt enough to fix up that old place can handle a little phone callin' and agenda planning. I'll get in touch with you."

Jack had served a couple of not-to-be-forgotten terms on Oklahoma's Economic Advisory Commission with Mildred. He was about to warn Sabrina of what she was really stepping into when another hearty thump on his back sent him forward a pace.

"I'm supposed to officially kick off this shindig in a few minutes," the mayor boomed. "Why don't you join me on the podium and say a few words. You can be the first to try out that fancy new sound system we bought with this year's donation from Wentworth Oil Works...assuming LeRoy can figure out how to work all those levers and dials, of course."

Since Mildred's husband, Dr. LeRoy Boyd, had taught aeronautical engineering at OU until his retirement some years ago, Jack had every confidence in his abilities to work the new PA system. He also knew darn well that if he got up on a stage with Sapulpa's mayor, the high school glee club, the reigning Mrs. Oklahoma, and every local politician up for reelection this coming November, he'd be stuck there for an hour or more.

"I'll pass, Mildred," he said easily. "I'm just here to enjoy myself tonight."

Her lively black eyes cut to Sabrina. "So I see, boy. So I see."

Thankfully, a harried committee member claimed the mayor's attention at that moment. Jack made a quick escape with Sabrina before they were both put to work solving whatever crisis was at hand.

"I'll call Mildred and get you out of working that rally if you want," he offered. "Just because she lives, breathes and eats projects like that, she thinks everyone else should, too."

"So I noticed," Sabrina replied, laughing. "Actually, I think I'd enjoy it." Her face tipped to his, the smile still in place. "And just for the record, I don't need you to get me out of the project if I didn't want to do it. I can fight my own battles, Jack."

"I'll remember that."

The easy response sent a tiny thrill down Sabrina's spine. For the second time in less than an hour, a hazy image of the future teased at the edges of her mind. A future that possibly, just possibly, included Jack Wentworth. Firmly, she reined in her skittering thoughts. The future would take care of itself. Tonight, she simply intended to enjoy the festival...and Jack.

She soon discovered that the mayor wasn't the only person in Sapulpa who knew her escort. Although he insisted on keeping a low profile, a number of the festival organizers went out of their way to thank him for his continuing support. At one point, the director of the local nursing home grabbed his arm and broke down in tears when she described the new TVs and computerized medicine dispensing system bought with a grant from Wentworth Oil. Gallantly, Jack passed her his handkerchief, then steered Sabrina toward some picnic tables set up under a spreading oak tree.

"I don't know about you," he muttered, "but I need a beer."

"Sounds good to me."

As they neared the tables, the scent of simmering barbecue evoked a loud rumbling from the vicinity of Sabrina's middle.

"How about a beer *and* some ribs?" Jack amended with a lift of one brow.

"Sounds even better."

After feasting on beans, cole slaw and baby back ribs so succulent that the blackened meat dropped off the bone in big chunks, they nursed a couple of long-necks through most of the speechifying. Later, they wandered through the art displays set up in the high school auditorium. Sculpture, wood carving, pottery, photography and paintings in every medium vied for attention in the juried displays.

Sabrina exclaimed over a small set of watercolors of old Route 66 roadside attractions, but refused Jack's offer to purchase them for her. He did convince her to accept a whimsical print of the Catoosa whale, however. She agreed only because all proceeds from the sale of the print went to the preservation of the two-story blue behemoth, an icon of the days when tacky attractions like rattlesnake farms and trading posts and gen-u-ine teepee motor courts stretched all along Route 66.

In return, Sabrina cajoled Jack into posing with her in front of a cardboard cutout of a sixties era twosome speeding along the famous Mother Road. After a to-ken protest, Jack agreed. Two minutes later, the pho-tographer slid the Polaroid shots into cardboard hold-ers preprinted with the date and the event, then handed one to each of them. Grinning, Sabrina paid for the pictures, handed him one copy, and added hers to the rolled-up whale print sticking out of her shoul-der bag.

By the time they exited the auditorium, the sun shimmered just above the horizon and the slow, se-ductive strains of Patsy Cline's "Crazy" drifted from the roped off area on Main Street.

"Now that's a song I recognize," Jack said. "Care to risk serious damage to your sandals, not to mention your bare toes, by dancing with me, Ms. Jensen?"

"I've got tough toes, Mr. Wentworth. It would be my pleasure."

Sabrina didn't realize the truth of that sentiment until they joined the throng of slow-moving dancers and Jack's arm slid around her waist. Dancing with him generated more than mere pleasure. Her pulse caught, then sped off when he brought her close against him. Small sparks ignited every time his breath brushed her temple. To Sabrina's consternation, his body also raised ripples of pure sensation everywhere it contacted hers.

She might have made it through the slow, dreamy number in one piece, though, if Jack's hand hadn't roamed from her waist to the bare skin of her back. Every nerve in her body leaped at his touch. Her throat went tight and dry. Her head came back, and her gaze met his.

Jack was still trying to handle the sensations roused by the feel of Sabrina's warm flesh under his fingertips when she leaned back a bit. Her green eyes shimmered, and he could no more resist licking the tiny spot of tangy sauce from the corner of her lips than he could stop the moon from glowing where it peeked above the storefronts.

A lick wasn't enough, of course. He had to have another taste. His mouth covered hers in a light, lingering kiss. Despite the deliberate casualness of the touch, white lightning streaked from his groin to his gut, then shot straight to his brain.

Jack raised his head, breathing hard. For a moment,

his nerves snapped like an exposed electrical wire. Every muscle in his body tensed with the need to crush her against him before reality came crashing in.

What in God's name was he doing?

Yesterday, he'd been pumping pure adrenaline from the brawl outside the diner. The kiss he'd stolen from Sabrina had kept him awake longer than he wanted to admit last night. But this instant, electrical response to her taste and her feel shocked him.

Dammit, hadn't he learned his lesson with Heather? He'd better back off, and quickly, before things went too far, too fast for either of them. Reluctantly, he disengaged. Not enough to release her. Just enough to put some breathing space between them.

"I'm sorry."

She didn't make any effort to hide her surprise.

"I shouldn't have done that," he said with a small, rueful smile.

"Why not?"

He was starting to get used to her directness.

"I told you last night I wasn't looking for more than a few hours spent in the company of an intriguing woman."

Her chin went up a degree or two. "That's right, you did."

"I don't want you to think I was blowing hot air through my hat, Sabrina, or that I'm trying to push you."

"I don't push easy."

Too late, he saw that he'd scratched her pride.

Again! With a look that would strip the threads from a rusty pipe, she pulled out of his arms.

"I guess I didn't make myself clear last night. I'm not interested in anything serious at this point in my life, either."

She turned away. Jack was still kicking himself for his clumsiness when he caught her low mutter.

"Especially not with a too handsome playboy whose ego is apparently a whole lot bigger than his granddaddy's stock portfolio."

He tried valiantly to recover, but the air between them remained cool until he drove Sabrina home a few hours later.

She didn't invite him in.

Chapter 6

Keeping an eye on the thinning Tuesday morning breakfast crowd, Sabrina leaned her shoulders against the wall of the diner's steamy kitchen and twisted a limp strand of hair around her forefinger.

"I'm fine, Rachel. Honestly."

Her twin snorted into the phone. "You don't sound fine. You sound like you're running yourself into the ground with work and school and that ridiculous schedule you've set for yourself to buy the diner."

"It's not ridiculous. If I swing the small business loan I've applied for, I can take over from Hank at the first of the year."

Rachel didn't respond, but Sabrina read her thoughts as clearly as if they were face to face. The sisters didn't talk to each other every day. They didn't need to. With the uncanny telepathy of twins, they communicated over long distances and extended time periods without words.

Right now, Sabrina knew, her sister was biting her lip. Rachel didn't share her sister's need for stability. Content to flit from job to job the same way she flitted from man to man, Rachel had inherited their father's optimistic outlook on life and their mother's inability or unwillingness to settle down. Sabrina worried about her constantly and, at moments like this, envied her.

"Why don't you come down to Oklahoma City this weekend?" her twin suggested. "We'll go skinny-dipping in the pool here at the apartments, like we did that night daddy left us at the motel to go next door and have a beer."

"We were seven years old then."

"So?"

"So I think twice about baring my behind in public these days. So should you. As best I recall, those jeans you borrowed from me stretched a bit tight across the rear."

"Buck likes them that way," Rachel purred.

"Buck?"

"The new guitarist at In Cahoots. Remember, I told you about him? Big, brawny and sooo—"

"Beautiful. Yes, I remember."

Smiling, Sabrina listened while her twin gave a quick update on her campaign to make the newest band member her love slave. Rachel estimated that it

would take another week of sashaying past and lean-
ing over to take orders at the noisy, cavernous coun-
try-western saloon and dance hall where she tended
bar. Sabrina gave the hapless Buck another night—
two at most.

"What about you?" Rachel probed. "Anything
happening with that rigger you told me about?"

Sabrina hesitated. Her sister had called the diner
just after Jack and his friend, Al, had left last week.
Convinced at the time that the mighty Jack Wentworth had been playing games with her, Sabrina had
told Rachel only that there had been a brawl and that
a certain long-legged rigger had promised to come
back later. She hadn't spoken to her sister since that
call.

Nor had she spoken to Jack in the past three and a
half days...not that she was counting.

"No," she answered with a mental shrug, "nothing's happening."

"Didn't he come back to the diner?"

"He did, but..."

"But you torched him," Rachel finished on a note
of disgust. "Come on, Sabrina, admit it. Every time
some guy gets too close to you or acts like he might
interfere with that almighty schedule you've set for
yourself, you push him away."

Sabrina wasn't ready to admit anything, especially
the fact that she hadn't exactly pushed Jack away. She
wasn't sure why she hesitated to talk about Jack
Wentworth to her inquisitive sister, or even share his

name. She was still too confused by her reaction to the man—and by his abrupt withdrawal the night of the Blowout—to discuss him at all, even with her twin.

"Look who's talking," she joked instead. "The minute ol' Buck shows the first signs of real interest, you'll cut him off at the knees."

"I'm just not ready to settle down. You, on the other hand, are *too* settled. You need to shake it up a bit. Let yourself go. Buy something short and slithery and outrageous—"

"So you can borrow it."

"...and have yourself a fling or two before you start building your empire of diners," Rachel concluded, ignoring her sister's dry interjection.

"Hey, I'm not exactly withering on the vine, you know. I've had a fling or two in my time."

"Ha! Those boys don't count. You need a man, twin. A real man. One who'll sweep you off your feet and rattle your bones and make you forget how to breathe."

That came too darn close to the mark for Sabrina's comfort. Tucking the limp strand into the twist at the back of her head, she pushed away from the wall.

"We'll continue this fascinating discussion some other time, okay? Hank's just come in, and I want to talk to him about restoring the old neon sign over the front door."

"If you put as much effort into your love life as

you do into your studies and that diner," her twin groused, "you'd…"

"I have to go. Talk to you soon."

Hanging up on her indignant sister, Sabrina cornered Hank in the tiny room at the back of the diner that served as a combination storeroom and office. Her first week at the diner, she'd rolled up her sleeves, waded in, and arranged the jumble of cans, boxes and sacks into reasonable order. In the months since, Hank had gradually turned over more and more of the inventory and bookkeeping tasks to Sabrina. She'd learned to account for his habit of dipping into the till whenever someone needed more than just a free meal. She'd even coaxed him into keeping an inventory sheet of sorts to save extra trips to their wholesale supplier. She hadn't quite convinced him to go along with her latest project, however—restoring the double-sided neon sign over the diner's front entrance.

Hank insisted that the peeling paint and blacked-out letters gave the place an air of authenticity, but Sabrina winced every time she pulled into the parking lot. With everything else that had needed fixing at the diner, she'd put the sign on the back burner. A peek at the prices of the neon art at the Blowout on Friday night, however, had convinced her that prices were only going to go up. She'd done some serious pencil pushing over the weekend. A few earnest phone calls yesterday had reworked the investment necessary to restore the sign to its original glory.

"Got a minute, Hank?"

"Maybe." He eyed her suspiciously and rolled the ever present cigar around in his mouth. "Why?"

Sabrina pulled out the revised sheet of figures she'd worked so hard on. "I called around for more estimates on restoring the sign."

"Oh, no. Not that again."

He turned, reaching for one of the five-pound sacks of kidney beans that went into his chili. Sabrina got between him and the beans.

"Just look at the figures. The best estimate I got was fifteen hundred dollars to spray paint the metal and retube the neon."

"Fifteen hundred!"

"We can save three hundred of that by taking the sign down ourselves and transporting it into Tulsa."

"That's still more'n we can afford."

"It would be," she agreed, "if our soft drink distributor hadn't promised to cough up another two hundred."

"Why the hell did he do that?"

"Because I convinced him that he should pay for the free advertising he'll get with his product's logo lit up in our sign," Sabrina disclosed, her eyes twinkling. "So what do you think? Should we do it?"

He scratched his shiny bald head. "Damn, woman, you're peskier than a flea at a dog reunion."

"Is that a yes or a no?"

"Yes, no, whatever," Hank grumbled. "You know

darn well you're gonna nag me until I agree, so you might as well do what you want.''

Sabrina suffered a momentary pang of conscience. A thousand dollars was a big investment, even with the sign maker's agreement to let them pay out the amount in manageable monthly installments.

''I'm sure we'll recoup the investment within six months. I did a cost benefit analysis using the Reimer statistical curve for advertising.'' She smoothed the folded papers with her palms. ''Look, if you enter the current customer base here and the minimum expected...''

A sound that was halfway between a wheeze and a chortle burst from Hank.

''Just go for it, Sabrina,'' he instructed with a flap of a gnarled hand. ''I don't trust book figures farther than I can spit 'em, but I trust your instincts.''

She refolded the papers, her smile wide and bright. ''Good. I asked a couple of our regulars to stop by this afternoon and help me take down the sign... assuming you agreed.''

Hank didn't even bother to respond to that.

''If you'll let me borrow your truck, I'll drive into Tulsa this afternoon,'' she said happily.

Reenergized, she went out front to wipe down the tables. This project was exactly what she needed to push Jack Wentworth out of her mind. Not that he'd occupied it exclusively during the past three and a half days. Just enough to annoy her.

Why in the world should it bother her that he

hadn't called or stopped by, anyway? She hadn't expected him to. Their Friday night excursion to Sapulpa had started out friendly enough—

Ha! Who was she kidding? Friday night had started out like a dream. Squirting a long arc of cleaner, Sabrina attacked a table. Her nose twitched from the disinfectant as she scrubbed.

She'd enjoyed everything about the first part of the evening, she admitted grudgingly. Right up to and including that dreamy dance and even dreamier kiss. So why had Jack pulled back? And why the heck had she gotten so bent out of shape when he did?

Maybe Rachel was right. Maybe Sabrina did take everything too seriously, including Jack Wentworth. Maybe she shouldn't worry so much about his agenda. In retrospect, she probably shouldn't have fired up at him the way she had. What was it he'd said? That he only wanted a few hours of her company?

Well, he got them, she thought. They had some fun, then went their separate ways. No expectations or promises on either side. She slapped her sponge onto a cracked Formica tabletop and tried—again—to convince herself that was exactly the way she wanted it.

By the time her recruits showed up to help take down the sign, Sabrina had scrubbed the tables, the floors and the bathrooms, then worked a busy noon rush. She should have felt drained, but her excitement bubbled like carbonated water as they went to work.

Grunting, her helpers attacked the rusted mounting assembly. One bolt after another came loose with a loud, protesting squeal. The sign loosened, then tipped drunkenly to one side.

"Careful!"

Directing the operation from the ground, Sabrina paced and peered and chewed anxiously on her lower lip. The pulley the men had rigged to lower the double-sided marquee into Hank's truck groaned and creaked. The sign swung farther to the right, over-corrected to the left, almost hit the side of the truck. Sabrina's heart stopped, then restarted with a kick when the marquee finally settled on a thick mat of folded pads.

"The eagle has landed," she crowed.

"Some eagle," one of the volunteers scoffed. "Looks more like crow bait to me."

Admittedly, the sign's rusted metal struts, peeling paint and fly-speckled neon tubing appeared even scruffier up close and personal, but Sabrina pictured it clean and glowing. While her recruits secured the massive marquee with additional pads and ropes, she dashed back into the diner to grab her purse.

"I'll be back in a few hours," she called.

Hank waved a tattooed arm. "Take your time. Peg and I can handle the supper crowd."

Humming happily, she drove slow and easy all the way into the city. She could find her way around Tulsa well enough, but it took some time to locate the north-side brick warehouse that housed Brite Lites

Commercial Signs. The owner whistled when he saw
the condition of the proposed job. With a promise to
do his best, he called an assistant. Straining and cursing under their breath, they winched the sign out of
the truck bed.

Sabrina decided to take advantage of the light mid-
afternoon traffic on the way back. Humming along
with George Strait, she cut through the downtown
streets. Bright June sunshine shafted through the glass
towers of the business district. Between the tall skyscrapers nestled shops that displayed elegant summer
suits and Stetsons. Restaurants beckoned businessmen
and women for high-powered deals made over aged
beef and bourbon.

Someday, Sabrina mused as she braked for a red
light, she just might house her corporate headquarters
in one of these glass towers. Her gaze swept the main
plaza, decorated with sleek sculpture and lined with
peeling, white-trunked river birches. The light
changed from red to green. She'd started to hit the
gas when a discreet bronze plaque caught her eye.

Wentworth Oil Works.

She might not have stopped if a car hadn't angled
out of a parking space right ahead of her. On a whim,
Sabrina pulled into the empty spot. She had some
time on her hands. Hank had said he didn't need her.
She'd just take a peek at the lobby.

The electric doors whooshed open, and Sabrina
stepped out of the June heat into a climate-controlled,
light-filled atrium. Stunned, she drank in the beauty

like a desert traveler would the cool shade of an oasis. Everywhere she looked, brass gleamed. Fountains splashed. Remington bronzes and Russell oils took her breath away.

Mesmerized, Sabrina wandered inside for a closer look at the mural that filled the far wall. In four huge panels, the painting depicted the Glenpool oil field at its peak. The raw intensity of the colors dazzled her eye. Even more powerful was the awesome scope of the work.

Derricks dotted a landscape that seemed to stretch into infinity. A small city of tar paper shacks nestled among towers. Model Ts and flatbed trucks threw up clouds of dust as they cut across endless stretches of red earth pooled with glistening black puddles. An early version of the Wentworth logo, Sabrina saw, showed prominently on the truck sides.

Impressed and just a little intimidated, she turned to leave. She was halfway to the front entrance when the bell beside one of the elevators dinged. The gleaming brass doors slid open, and Jack Wentworth walked out.

A different Jack Wentworth, she saw with a gulp. Just as tall and broad-shouldered, but this time his shoulders were covered in hand-tailored charcoal gray gabardine. Just as handsome, but with the added edge of sophistication that comes with money and power.

"I think we should go after those leases," he was telling the suited executive with him. "The market is riding a wave right now, but I—"

He stopped abruptly. Surprise chased across his face, followed by a smile of genuine pleasure.

"Sabrina! Were you coming up to see me?"

Embarrassed, she fingered the strap to her shoulder bag. "No. I was in town on business and, uh, just happened to be passing by."

She winced inwardly. Talk about your basic lame excuses!

"Do you have time for a cup of coffee?"

His smile was warm and friendly, as though they hadn't parted with a decidedly cool goodbye three nights ago. Regaining her composure with an effort, Sabrina hitched her purse up higher on her shoulder.

"No, but thanks for the offer. You're on your way out and I—"

"I was just going out to look at some leases we plan to acquire." He sent the man beside him a quick glance. "We can reschedule, can't we, Don?"

"Sure." The older man's reply was easy enough, but his expression said clearly that he wasn't pleased. "I kept the owners dangling, though, while you were up in Alaska this weekend inspecting that pipeline. They called again yesterday, hoping for an answer when you got back this morning."

Alaska. That explained why he hadn't called her— not that she'd expected him to! Still, the smile she gave him came close to matching his.

"Please don't change your plans on my account. I, uh, have to get back anyway."

Another lame excuse, but he didn't need to know

that. His gaze roamed her face, sparking little pin-pricks of pleasure everywhere it touched. Without turning aside, he sent his associate off.

"Give us a minute, will you, Don?"

The older man nodded. "I'll wait for you in the limo."

While the broker's footsteps faded into the background, Jack drank in Sabrina's wide green eyes and full mouth. He'd thought about that mouth during the past three days. More than once! Hell, he'd had plenty of time during the long flight up and back from Alaska to think about every part of this prickly female. He'd arrived back in Tulsa early this morning, convinced he'd made the right move when he'd pulled back and attempted to put the skids on his growing fascination with her.

The fierce pleasure that had knifed through him when he'd caught sight of her a moment ago convinced him otherwise.

He'd take it slow, he swore. He wouldn't make any promises he couldn't keep, or let things get too deep, too fast. He wouldn't make the same mistake he'd made with Heather. But neither could he let Sabrina turn around and walk out of his building and his life.

"I planned to call you this week," he told her. "To apologize. I guess I came across sounding like a pompous ass the other night."

"As a matter of fact…"

His mouth kicked into a grin. She hadn't forgiven

him, but she was willing to let him grovel for a while. He took that as a positive sign.

"I'd suggest we start over again, but I've already tried that approach once."

"So, what approach are you going to try this time?"

"Something more direct. How about dinner tonight at the Petroleum Club?"

She hesitated, clearly tempted, then dragged out the age-old feminine lament.

"I don't think I'm appropriately dressed for dinner at that bastion of the rich and powerful."

In Jack's opinion, Sabrina in jeans and a stretchy knit tank top could walk into any room in any town in any country and knock its occupants right back on their heels. If he tried to tell her so, however, he'd no doubt come off sounding as patronizing or as pompous as he had the other night.

"You look fine to me, but we can go somewhere else if you'd prefer."

"Well…"

She nibbled on her lower lip for a moment. Jack swallowed, hard, and pulled his eyes from the wet satin of her mouth.

"My sister was on my case this morning about jazzing up my wardrobe. Maybe I'll do a little shopping while you're out grabbing up gas and oil leases."

Jack had the sense to keep his mouth shut. He'd felt the rough edge of Sabrina's pride a few times already. He knew darn well she'd chew him up and spit him out in small pieces if he offered to underwrite a visit to one of the exclusive and very expensive Tulsa boutiques that his sister, Josie, frequented.

"Would you like to use my office to change and freshen up after your shopping expedition?" he offered instead. "We can go to the club from here."

She flashed a quicksilver grin. "As long as I'm going to spend the rest of the afternoon in the big city, I might as well go for broke and get my hair done, too. I'll meet you at the Petroleum Club."

"Seven o'clock?"

"Fine."

Jack escorted Sabrina through the lobby and stood beside the waiting limo, watching as she hooked her purse over her shoulder and sauntered off. Her long, slender legs ate up the pavement, and her trim bottom caused more than one male head to turn when she passed. Jack's fingers tightened on the open car door.

They were only meeting for dinner, he reminded himself sternly. A drink or two, and dinner. Yet the thought of that dinner sent anticipation razoring right through him.

It was only dinner, Sabrina told herself fiercely as she paused before the window of a small, elegant shop two blocks from the Wentworth Building. Just a few hours in the company of a man she found...to use his own phrase...intriguing.

She was nuts even to *think* about going into a

pricey shop like this for a dress to wear for just a few hours...despite the fact that the little black number in the window fit Rachel's description exactly. It was short and slinky, and Sabrina didn't doubt the price tag carried a figure that was totally outrageous.

She couldn't afford a dress like that, even if they had it in her size, which they probably didn't. Any more than she could afford to squander the afternoon and most of the evening playing instead of working or studying. What's more, it was crazy to waste money on having her hair and nails done. The polish would only chip off tomorrow when she went back to her real world, and no stylist had ever been able to coax her heavy mane into anything more sophisticated than a loose topknot.

The arguments piled up in her head, one after another, then suddenly collapsed.

She couldn't afford that dress, but she *wanted* it. Almost as badly as she wanted to spend a few more hours in Jack's company. And while she was at it, she might as well admit that the budding entrepreneur in her would kill for a glimpse inside the Petroleum Club, where fortunes were made and lost over rare prime rib and aged bourbon.

What the heck!

Throwing caution and common sense to the winds, Sabrina dug in her wallet to make sure she had the charge card she normally reserved only for emergencies, then pushed open the dark green door and sailed inside.

The saleswoman—correction, sales *consultant,* according to her engraved brass name badge—smiled a greeting.

"May I help you?"

"I certainly hope so."

Chapter 7

The call came just as Jack was downing a long swallow of Scotch.

He'd arrived at the Petroleum Club with a good half hour to kill. He could have joined several of his friends in the casual lounge with its panoramic view of Tulsa's skyline. He could have used the offices set aside for patrons to make a few of his more pressing calls.

Instead, he'd opted to wait for Sabrina in the spacious reception area just off the elevators. The oversize leather chairs were every bit as comfortable and the view, while not quite as panoramic as that in the bar, showed the river winding like a rope of pure silver through the city.

Ignoring the discreetly placed TV screen that flickered with the latest stock market quotes, Jack stretched out his legs and raised the heavy crystal tumbler. The Scotch added its kick to the anticipation swirling in his gut. A vision of Sabrina as she'd appeared in the lobby of the Wentworth Building shimmered in his mind. Her hair a silky, windblown tumble. Her nose shiny. Her lips chewed bare of lipstick. And that fantastic, throat-closing body molded by stretchy knit and snug jeans.

A bolt of old-fashioned lust caught Jack right in the chest and headed south. He and Sabrina had hit a few rough spots the first couple of times they'd connected. He intended to see that didn't happen tonight. His fingers gripped the crystal tumbler. Tonight he'd—

"There's a call for you, Mr. Wentworth. Would you care to take it here or in the office?"

The crystal tumbler landed on the table with a thunk. Disappointment added a sharp, bitter tang to the taste of Scotch.

She'd backed out.

He'd half expected her to, but the knowledge that his on-again, off-again association with Sabrina Jensen had taken another hit tied a king-size knot in his gut. What *was* it about this woman?

Keeping his voice neutral, he identified himself. Relief arrowed through him when the irritated male at the other end of the line did the same.

"You didn't tell me you had laid on a trip to Alaska this weekend," Trey McGill complained.

Jack shook his head. After all these years, his State Department contact still stewed when real life impinged on the covert operations he coordinated. Trey had a tendency to forget that it was Wentworth business that provided Jack his cover...and his access to so many world leaders that the U.S. couldn't or wouldn't officially recognize.

"The trip came up suddenly," he replied evenly. "A section of pipeline sprung a leak, and I wanted to make sure the crews contained the spill before it caused serious environmental damage."

"Did you get my message?"

"Yes."

"Can you talk?"

He made a quick sweep of the reception area. Aside from a portly, gray-haired banker with his eyes glued to the stock market quotes, the place was empty.

"Yes."

"Hang on while I scramble the signal."

A slight buzz reverberated against Jack's eardrum, then Trey came back on. Crisply, he confirmed what he'd reported in his previous, coded message.

"We've come up with a complete bust. Neither the FBI nor CIA databases had anything on the two men who almost ran you and the prince down."

"What about the truck?"

"One fitting the description you gave us was reported stolen last year in Texas. Without the license plate number we couldn't confirm that it was the same vehicle."

He paused, and Jack could hear the faint tapping of a pen against a pad or notebook. That kind of nervous habit would give Trey away in a minute if he had to go undercover, Jack thought with a tight inner smile. Good thing McGill's role in these missions involved coordination and control, not field ops.

"We checked out everyone we could at the diner," the government agent reported, "including the owner and this Jensen woman."

"And?" Jack asked softly.

"And they look clean."

"*Look* clean, Trey?"

The tapping picked up speed.

"All right, they *are* clean, at least according to what we've turned up so far. But I'm not satisfied. I'm going to dig deeper, and harder…particularly in light of what's happening in Qatar."

Jack's gaze narrowed dangerously. Dammit! Trey had taken his sweet time getting around to the real point of this call.

"Cut to the meat," he ordered, annoyed and wanting McGill to know it. "What's happening in Qatar?"

"We just got a dispatch from our chief consul in country. It goes on for five pages of not-so-polite bureaucratese, but the essence is that he's fed up. He wants to know why the government he's supposed to represent cut him out of the loop by sending some kind of a secret deal back with the prince."

Jack came straight up in his chair, the phone hard

against his ear. He shot the banker another quick look and lowered his voice.

"How the hell did the consul find out about the accord? Ali swore his father would keep it under wraps until he and the rest of the Gulf Corporation Council leaders had a chance to look it over."

"Yeah, well, someone leaked it, either in Qatar or at this end. The details haven't surfaced yet, but rumors are thicker than flies over there. *El Jafir* has already started making nasty noises."

Jack swore, long and low. He'd tangled once before with the loose confederation of fundamental fanatics who called themselves *El Jafir*—the Wind. Determined to blow away the heretical outsiders with the same ferocity the hot winds blew the sands across the deserts, the group had attacked a remote drilling site jointly operated by the Sheikdom of Qatar and Wentworth Oil. Ali had retaken the site, aided by the arms and reinforcements Jack had personally brought in. The victory had raised the prince in his father's esteem. Unfortunately, it had also made him a target for increasingly vicious attacks by those who decried his close ties to the West.

"If *El Jafir* learns about your part in the secret accord, they'll go after something bigger than a drilling site in the middle of the desert," Trey predicted. "The refinery maybe, or one of Wentworth Oil's offshore rigs."

"I'll get word to our people to increase security," Jack said, his voice grim.

"In the meantime, we're putting together an emergency aid package for the emir. We're also trying to trace the source of the leak."

"Good idea."

The acid in the terse reply got to Trey.

"Hell, Jack, you know as well as I do that it could have come from anyone. Why do you think I wanted to check out those two drunks and the people at this diner you stopped at? Maybe the prince let something drop—"

"He didn't."

"He was trying to put the make on this Jensen woman, wasn't he?"

"She's a waitress, Trey, not an international terrorist."

"True, but who knows what the prince told her? Or what she told other people who may or may not have been tailing you?"

"Ali didn't tell her anything," Jack snapped. "I was with him the entire time, remember?"

Except, he remembered suddenly, for the few moments it had taken for him to retrieve his wallet from the dust beside his truck.

"I'm not saying Kaisal spilled anything he thought was significant to this woman," Trey argued, "but we both know how he lays it on when he's got a female in his gun sights. He probably promised to bury her in diamonds or paint her toenails with gold. Women seem impressed by that kind of thing," he added flatly.

"Some women," Jack agreed, refusing to duck the barb.

Heather hadn't made any secret of her fascination with the Wentworth wealth. Sabrina, on the other hand, had been totally unimpressed by both Ali's extravagant promises and Jack's family background.

Or had she?

Frowning, he stared at Tulsa's gold-tinted skyline. Like a video on fast forward, scenes from his on-again, off-again association with Sabrina Jensen flashed through his mind.

That first afternoon at the diner, she'd laughed off both his and Ali's bids for her attention...until the drunks had identified him as Jack Wentworth, he remembered, his stomach tightening. After that, she'd melted in his arms and invited him to her place that night.

Big deal. When he'd arrived at her house, she'd accused him of slumming and sent him off.

No, Jack corrected, he'd backed off...after inviting her to the Blowout, which she'd agreed to readily enough. The excursion had ended on a strained note, true, but not so strained that Jack hadn't intended to call Sabrina when he returned from Alaska.

Except she didn't wait for him to call her.

His jaw now as tight as his stomach, Jack recalled his surprise and fierce satisfaction when she'd appeared in the lobby this afternoon. She'd said she was just passing by—

Hell!

He was still calculating the odds of Sabrina "passing by" that particular building on the exact day he returned to Tulsa when the elevator doors opened.

"I'll call you later," he told Trey slowly. "I need to think about this a little more."

He dropped the phone into its cradle and rose, his intent gaze locked on the woman who stepped out of the elevator. She stood for a moment in the slanting rays of the sun, a silhouette of black silk and bare shoulders. The dress was the kind his sister, Josie, would describe as a stud stopper. Short, simple and sexy as hell, its neckline dived to a tantalizing promise in front and even deeper in back, Jack saw when she turned to the attendant. Her hair was swept up in a sophisticated French twist, and she carried herself with such unconscious, pulse-pounding sensuality that even the gray-haired banker abandoned his stock quotes to gape.

She caught sight of Jack just then, and a shy smile sprang into her eyes. A few moments ago, that curving mouth would have banished everything but the need to slide his hands up her bare back, destroy that smooth twist and kiss her until her bones melted. Now, doubt added a serrated edge to his lust.

He'd been in the business too long to let that doubt show in his face, but it took a whole lot more effort to keep it out of his voice than he liked.

"At the risk of sounding sexist as hell, may I say that you do things to that dress that should be declared illegal?"

"At the risk of sounding smug, thank you."

Despite her flip comeback, Jack's gruff compliment played havoc with Sabrina's nerves. The way his eyes seemed to eat at her from the inside out didn't exactly help matters, either.

She'd recovered from the shock of signing her name to a charge slip that would take her three months of extra shifts to pay off. She'd also managed to shrug aside the irony of having her hair shampooed and shaped by a stylist who, she'd discovered, owned a Mercedes and a winter retreat in Barbados. She'd even found herself enjoying the luxury of a valet to park Hank's beat-up truck and a swift ascension in a private elevator to this aerie of eagles.

She'd felt only a slowly mounting excitement, in fact, until she stepped off the elevator and caught sight of Jack. Now, she could barely remember her name.

He stopped just close enough to her side to raise the fine hairs on Sabrina's arms. The skin beneath shivered in delight. Or desire. At this point, she couldn't tell the difference.

"Are you hungry?"

She gulped, hoping the answer didn't flame on her face.

"Or would you like a drink first?"

"I'd better pass on that. I didn't have lunch. Alcohol does funny things to me on an empty stomach, and I still have to drive home tonight."

"Only if you want to."

Sabrina sucked air into suddenly collapsed lungs. She stared up at him, feeling every watt of the electricity in his glittering blue eyes.

"What happened to not pushing too hard or too fast?"

The voltage pegged another few marks on the meter. Sabrina figured she'd wear the scorch marks for the next month.

"I wasn't pushing, sweetheart. Just offering an option."

She started to suggest that he drop the sweetheart bit, as she had the first day he'd laid it on her. For some reason, the words wouldn't come out. Probably because she was starting to like the sound of it coming from Jack. Or maybe because her whole back from her heels to her hair caught fire when he put his hand at her waist to guide her into the dining room.

She recovered in time to smile at the waiter holding out her chair. Plucking the napkin folded into the shape of an oil derrick off the snowy linen, the server laid it across her lap. The menu he handed her gave no prices. For a moment, Sabrina ascribed that omission to a chauvinism that went even deeper than the bank accounts of the club's exclusive membership. Then she realized that only members could pay for the meals consumed here.

Not that money ever changed hands at the club, she guessed, glancing around. These captains of the oil industry wouldn't be so crass as to actually count out their bills in public. They probably didn't even

sign the chit, simply trusted the century-old establishment to forward a bill each month for food, drinks
and the cigars displayed in a climate-controlled glass
humidor right next to the largest, most gorgeous arrangement of bloodred gladiolas Sabrina had ever
seen. Tall crystal vases holding individual stems of
the same flowers graced the edge of each table, giving
the diners an illusion of privacy.

The waiter took their order for iced tea and disappeared. Jack didn't bother to open his menu.

"I can recommend the prime rib."

"Why doesn't that surprise me?"

Grinning, Sabrina skimmed the entrees, which con-
sisted of beef, beef and more beef. Ah! At the bottom
of the second page were a few fish and game dishes
for the clogged arteries in the club.

"Nothing on the menu can compare to that hamburger you dished up at the diner," he told her, "but
the prime rib is cooked over a mesquite fire."

"That's good enough for me!"

The waiter reappeared at almost the same instant
the embossed leather menu snapped shut. When
they'd both placed their orders, Jack picked up the
conversation.

"You said you were in town this afternoon on business," he said casually. "I was too glad to see you
to ask what kind of business."

"I brought the sign in for restoration, the one from
over the diner's front door."

"Good Lord. That thing must weigh a ton!"

"Closer to a ton and a half."

"How'd you get it down?"

"A couple of our regulars helped."

"Is there enough left of it to restore?"

"According to Brite Lites, there is."

Jack cocked his head, his eyes thoughtful. "From what I understand, neon is an expensive art form. Won't it take a lot of onion burgers and smothered steak to restore a sign that large?"

Sabrina crossed her forearms on the table and hunched forward, secretly pleased at being able to share the details of her long-planned project with someone who would understand them.

"I whittled down some of the cost by hauling the thing into the shop myself. I also got our soft drink distributor to kick in for his free advertising once the sign is restored."

She was so caught up in relating her coup that she almost missed the quick slide southward Jack's gaze took. Too late, she realized that a hunch wasn't the best position to assume in this dress. She leaned back, her face warming as the black silk settled in more discreet folds over her breasts.

Jack's eyes cut back to her face. He made no apology for enjoying the scenery, but he saved his skin by not commenting on it.

"So the sign brought you to Tulsa," he said with a composure that had deserted Sabrina. "What brought you into the building?"

"The Wentworth Building?"

No way was she going to admit to prurient curiosity over anything and everything about Jack Wentworth. Her shoulders lifted in a small shrug.

"I told you. I was just passing by and decided to take a peek."

"That's right. You did tell me."

His slow drawl held no trace of amusement or disbelief, but Sabrina wouldn't have blamed him for either. Next time, she vowed, she would have *some* excuse handy for tracking a man down to his home lair. Thankfully, their salads arrived at that moment, accompanied by a gold-weave basket giving off heavenly hot dough smells. She sniffed appreciatively as the waiter placed a crusty dinner roll on her bread plate, followed by a pat of pale golden butter decorated with the club's crest.

She did her best not to wolf down the butter-drenched roll, but it took some doing. The diner didn't come close to turning out bread this crusty on the outside and so exquisitely soft on the inside. She chewed, swallowed, and contemplated the wire basket for a moment. Deciding to save herself for the feast to follow, she turned her head to contemplate Jack instead.

"I forgot to ask you the other night. Did your friend Al get home okay?"

Casually, he buttered a man-size hunk of roll. "Why do you think he was on his way home?"

The question stumped her. She stared at him blankly for a moment, thinking back.

"I don't know. I guess because he kept trying to convince me to fly off to Qatar with him. I assumed he meant then, not sometime in the indeterminate future. Where the heck is Qatar, anyway?"

"It's a small country, just a spur of the Arabian Peninsula that juts into the Persian Gulf."

That didn't tell her a whole lot. She and Rachel had traveled a good bit in their years on the road with their father. They'd since taken a couple of trips to Mexico and one to Saskatchewan, but hadn't quite made it to the Arabian Peninsula. From the extensive TV coverage of the Gulf War, though, she retained a mental image of a huge, hazy triangle dominated primarily by Saudi Arabia and Iraq, with the tiny Kuwait caught between.

"So did Al get wherever he was going in one piece? No further run-ins with drunken riggers?"

"No, no further run-ins."

"Good. What about you? What took you to Alaska?"

Sabrina sneaked another roll and popped a warm, unbuttered chunk into her mouth. A full mouth was one way to stop the questions rolling out of her like trucks off an assembly line, she thought with an inner grimace.

Okay, so she was curious. She and Jack had done more eating and dancing than talking the night of the Blowout. Unfortunately, the dancing had ended abruptly when she'd pulled out of his arms, and the talking never quite resumed after that.

Even more to the point, this suited executive bore so little resemblance to the lean-hipped rigger who'd driven up to…and away from…her house that night that she felt just a bit off balance. Or maybe it was the way his eyes cut into her tonight, as though he were seeing someone he, too, found totally different.

Jack's reply banished the odd notion. His voice was easy, his answer relaxed. "I went up to check out a leak in one of our pipelines."

"Uh-oh."

"Our people had it contained, but we're testing some new microbe absorbents. I wanted to see how well the little critters gobbled up the spill."

As he related the details of his trip, Jack felt the tension in the muscles at the back of his neck imperceptibly ease. If Sabrina was pumping him for information, she was about as subtle as a steel bit augering through solid rock. He couldn't convince himself that she was playing the same dangerous game he and Trey had played for so many years.

Dammit, he'd lived parts of his life in the shadows for so long he was starting to see ghosts where there were none. Unless his instincts had taken a serious wrong turn in the past few days, the woman sitting opposite him had nothing to do with the attack by the two supposed drunks. Or with the rumors starting to surface about Ali's visit to the United States. What's more, Sabrina had disclosed a legitimate reason for coming into the city today, if not into the Wentworth Building.

That Jack ascribed to the same chemistry that had kept his nerves doing their own version of a two-step since the moment he'd laid eyes on her. The dance tempo picked up considerably each time his gaze drifted to the curve of her breasts displayed so enticingly by that invitation to sin she was wearing.

By the time their dinner arrived, Jack had forced himself to fully relax. Watching Sabrina demolish her dinner helped the process considerably. She didn't play coy when it came to food, he noted with the first hint of real amusement since Trey's phone call. If he remembered correctly, she'd packed away as many ribs as he had the night of the Blowout. She dug into her prime rib with the same unabashed appreciation.

Carving the two-inch thick slab of aged beef with the skill of someone who knew her way around a sharp knife, she savored each morsel. Jack, in turn, found himself savoring the laughter that came into her eyes when the talk turned from oil-gobbling microbes to the OSU Cowboy's chances for another winning season, to family in general and siblings in particular.

"Mine lives in Oklahoma City," Sabrina told him between bites of prime rib, reinforcing the information Jack had already received. "We're twins, but it's hard to believe we erupted from the same gene pool."

"Let me guess. She isn't into Woody Guthrie and old neon signs."

Her eyes lit with a combination of exasperation and love. "Rachel isn't into anything that lasts longer than a coat of nail polish, including but not limited to jobs, residences and men.''

"Sounds a lot like my younger brother, Michael,'' Jack said dryly. "He claims he likes to keep his options open.''

"That's one way of putting it, I suppose.''

She pushed the remainder of the prime rib around on her plate. There wasn't enough left for two ticks to make a meal of.

"Rachel and I pretty much grew up on the road with our dad. She still has road tar in her blood.''

"And you don't?''

"Nope. I'm happy right where I am, up to my elbows in onion burgers. I'll be even happier when I finish my degree and take over the diner from Hank.''

"The first in your chain of Route 66 eateries stretching from Chicago to Santa Monica.''

"Or at least from Tulsa to Oklahoma City,'' she replied, grinning.

"Speaking of which, I saw something today that might interest you.'' Jack leaned forward, offering the treat he'd been saving for the right moment. "One of the long-term leases I looked at this afternoon includes a dilapidated old motel on the property. It's vintage thirties, on a stretch of broken asphalt that used to be the Mother Road. The owner wants us to bulldoze the buildings and clean up the land as part of a package deal.''

"Oh, no! What a shame we can't save old landmarks like that!''

"From what I saw, this one's gone well beyond saving. I'd guess that the roofs caved in on most of the cabins two decades ago. But I can put you in touch with the owner if you want to root around for any salvageable items before we plow the place down."

She sat up straight, her face alive with the thrill of the hunt. "Would you?"

"I'll call you tomorrow with the information."

He should have known her prickly pride would kick in.

"Make sure the owner understands I'm willing to pay for anything I find."

"He'd probably pay *you* to cart it off."

"I don't want any favors," she insisted stubbornly. "I'll negotiate with him for any bits and pieces I salvage."

Jack lifted both palms, conceding the point, and settled back to watch as she polished off the last of her dinner. A few moments later she sat back with another sigh, this one of utter repletion.

While the waiter poured coffee, her glance roamed the dining room. It had filled in the past hour. The hum of conversations that had carried from the board-room to the bar to the table rose above rattling cutlery and the clink of ice against glass.

Her eyes grew thoughtful. Determination settled like a mask over her features as she sipped her coffee and took in the power deals being brokered all around her. For a moment, Jack caught a remarkable resemblance between Sabrina of the creamy skin and silky hair and the gruff, irreverent, irascible old pirate who was his grandfather.

They'd get along, he thought with a hitch in his gut. Like Sabrina, Joseph Wentworth had decided to put his roots down in Oklahoma soil. In Joseph's case, that soil had subsequently oozed black. The old man had lived, breathed and slept the oil and gas business for sixty years. He'd never understood his grandson's restlessness, had roared like a lion with a thorn stuck in its gums when Jack had decided on a stint in the navy after graduating from college. Nor did he know about the secret, often dangerous tasks Jack now performed for the government. He sure as hell wouldn't be happy about them if he did.

Sabrina wouldn't understand the hidden slice of his life either, Jack suspected. Unlike her twin, she craved stability. Security. Something to anchor her firmly in the world she intended to create for herself.

She'd build her string of diners. Jack didn't have any doubt. Like his grandfather, she knew exactly what she wanted and was going after it. He was just making a mental note to quietly grease the financial skids for her when she took a final sip from her coffee cup and brought her gaze back to his.

"Thanks for dinner, Jack, and for the chance to rub elbows with the movers and the shakers. If I want to join your ranks, I'd better hit the road, then hit the books. I've got an early class tomorrow."

"No dessert?"

"I couldn't stuff down another bite."

"No more coffee?"

"Uh-uh, but thanks."

"No going back to my place for a couple of hours of hot, mindless sex?"

"Maybe next time," she replied, not missing a beat as she reached for her purse.

The quick comeback had him sucking in a sharp breath. He'd thrown out that line as a joke. Well, partly as a joke. He hadn't exactly sat through dinner planning ways to jump Sabrina's bones, although the thought had occurred to him once or twice... especially when she'd leaned forward to make a point. Between that killer dress and the insidious doubts planted by Trey's call, Jack couldn't remember when he'd enjoyed a steak less.

Now that dinner was over and his doubts were laid to rest, he discovered that he wanted dessert. Badly. And when Sabrina freshened her lipstick, leaving her mouth red and glossy and so damned inviting, his want shot into hot, driving need.

He rose, his body tight, and pulled out her chair. His pulse hammered at every pressure point as he escorted her to the elevator. Before the door glided shut, he had his hands braced on either side of her head.

"Any chance I can change your mind?"

"About the coffee or the sex?"

"Either one."

She flicked a glance over his shoulder at the elevator's indicator panel. "You've got sixteen floors to give it your best shot."

He gave it his best shot.

His mouth came down, hard and hungry. Hers came up, hot and eager. He didn't surge forward, didn't crush her against the wood paneling with his body, but the fierce urge to do just that generated a heat that scorched the air in the small, paneled cage.

By the tenth floor, the fire in his blood ignited.

By the fifth, he was hard as a rock.

By the time the elevator stopped at the underground parking level, he knew he didn't want a couple of hours of hot, mindless sex with this woman. He wanted it sweet and so slow that she would weep before they were done. Hell, he was close to weeping himself.

The doors whirred open. The valet started their way, gaped for a moment, then grinned and retreated to his counter with its pegboard full of keys.

"Change your mind?" Jack murmured, following the curve of her flushed cheek with his mouth.

She tried to answer. Swallowed. Tried again.

"Almost."

He trapped a groan in his chest, pulled back to look down at her.

"I want to," she whispered. "So badly it hurts. But we said no strings, remember? No wading in too fast or too deep. If I go home with you now, I have a feeling I'll be in way, way over my head."

She left him with another brief kiss and the bitter taste of his own words in his mouth. About the only satisfaction Jack got from the moment was that her green eyes shimmered with regret.

Chapter 8

Sabrina was right.

Another hour—hell, another few minutes—and they both would have plunged right off the deep end. Jack acknowledged that stark fact, accepted it, fought it all during the drive to the sprawling Wentworth estate in Freemont Springs, some miles west of Tulsa.

Alone in the heavy darkness of the summer night, with the concrete whirring under the Jag's tires and every muscle in his body aching with unrelenting need, he could admit that Sabrina Jensen had become a hunger, a thirst. He wanted her. He craved her. No woman had ever tied him in so many knots. Unless he wanted to stay that way, Jack decided grimly, he'd better put the tantalizing, green-eyed waitress from his mind.

Yeah, right. As if he could.

Gritting his teeth, he tried to concentrate on the two-lane country road, on the call from Trey, on the situation in Qatar. On anything but the regret in Sabrina's eyes when she walked away from him tonight.

Trey's call certainly gave him plenty to think about. The news that dissident factions in Qatar had already heard rumors of the secret accord Ali carried back with him worried Jack. Big time. He'd been in the business long enough to know that once rumors began circulating, trouble soon followed.

Reaching for his cell phone, he made a quick call to the Wentworth twenty-four-hour operations center. The senior controller on duty was an engineer and an old field hand. Like Jack, he'd learned the business the hard way. He didn't question the instructions to heighten security at the Wentworth operational sites in Qatar.

"Consider it done, Jack."

"Call me if anything breaks over there."

"You got it."

By the time the high stone wall encircling the thousand-acre estate Joseph Wentworth had carved out of the Oklahoma hills appeared in the headlights, the hard stroke of Jack's pulse had slowed. He couldn't seem to shake his biting regret at having let Sabrina walk away, though. It stayed in his thoughts as he pulled up to the massive wrought-iron front gates. Infrared sensors picked up the signal from the transmitter installed under the Jag's hood. Like silent, well-trained sentinels, the huge gates slid open, then shut once more.

A sense of coming home settled over Jack as he swept up the long drive. He knew every curve and turnout along the quarter-mile approach to the main house. He and his younger brother and sister had even named each of the graceful statues tucked into picturesque alcoves at strategic viewpoints.

The stables appeared first, a long low building of native stone covered with ivy. Then the garages with attached chauffeur's quarters and the artist's studio. Tucked into a grove of towering elms was the two-story stone butler's cottage that had been converted into a guest house some years ago.

Gravel spit under the Jag's tires as it passed the cottage and headed for the sprawling, three-story main house. Constructed of native stone quarried on the estate and cut with a diamond-bladed saw, the mansion sat atop a rolling rise. In daylight, it commanded a panoramic view of the five interlocking man-made lakes that surrounded it like the moat of a medieval castle. On a moonlit night such as this, the pale gray walls rose like ghostly battlements out of the velvety darkness.

Joseph had spared no expense in the construction of his palace. New York architects, Italian stonecutters, English wood-carvers and Japanese gardeners had all contributed to the unique style Jack privately dubbed Oklahoma baroque. In addition to housing a priceless collection of Western art, the thirty-two room, three-story mansion had his grandfather's personality stamped all through it. A bas relief over the front entrance immortalized his first gusher. Two of his favorite hunting dogs curled in eternal marble slumber on either side of the huge fireplace in his bedroom. The swimming pool in the basement replicated the shape of the state of Oklahoma.

Most people would have called the mansion an outrageous, egocentric monument to a self-made man. After their parents were lost in a boating accident, Jack and his younger sister and brother called it home. They still did, although he and Josie maintained separate residences for those times when their grandfather grew too overbearing and irascible…a not unfrequent occurrence.

After pulling up under a massive porte cocherie at the side entrance, Jack climbed out of the Jag. Immediately, the summer night surrounded him, as hot and humid as a saddle blanket. He left the keys in the car and took the shallow stone steps in two long strides.

He didn't worry about anyone driving off in the Jag. After a would-be kidnapper broke into the mansion in the early '60s, Joseph had insisted on the latest state-of-the-art security systems. Jack saw that they were upgraded every year to accommodate new advances in technology. No one entered…or left…the Wentworth estate undetected.

His footsteps echoing on the black-and-white terrazzo tiles, Jack strode down the vaulted hallway to the staircase that branched in graceful curves to the upper story. He'd almost reached the sanctuary of his second-floor bedroom-office when his grandfather's voice boomed from the master suite at the east end of the hall.

"Is that you, Jack?"

The crusty old oilman's heart might stutter and skip a few beats on occasion, but he had the hearing of a hungry coyote.

"It is."

"'Bout time you showed your face around here," Joseph grumbled as Jack strolled into his sitting room.

His grandfather was ensconced in his favorite chair, a half-empty glass of bourbon on the table beside him. His face retained its ruddy hue under a full mane of salt-and-pepper hair. His brown eyes were keen as he raked his grandson with a searching glance.

"Where've you been, boy?"

"I went out to look at those leases we talked about, then had dinner at the Petroleum Club."

"That so? Are they serving up raw steak at the Club these days?"

"Not that I noticed. Why?"

"Either you dribbled steer juice down your chin or you've been kissing someone partial to red lipstick."

Unruffled, Jack pulled a folded handkerchief from his pocket. When he offered no explanation of the smear, his grandfather's bushy eyebrows lifted.

"Does that brand on your chin come from the same woman you took to the Blowout last Friday night?"

"How did you know I went to the Blowout?"

Neither time nor hard living had diminished his grandfather's barreling laugh. It rolled up from his belly, as it always had, and won an answering grin from Jack, as it always did.

"I have my ways, boy, I have my ways."

"You've been pumping Hannah for information again, haven't you?"

"Ha! Since when do I have to rely on that she-mule who calls herself your housekeeper for my information? And don't try to side-rail me. Just answer the question."

"Yes, it was the same woman."

"Who is she?"

"No one you know."

"GoodLordawmighty, I hope not! Every female of my acquaintance is pushing seventy. Except those twits your brother brings home on occasion," Joseph muttered. "More hair than brains, every one of 'em, and a whole lot more chest than hair."

Snaking out a fist that showed the marks of age and a good number of barroom brawls, Joseph snagged his glass and tossed back the rest of his drink. The bourbon didn't mellow him. If anything, it had the opposite effect. His shaggy brows lowering, he launched into his favorite theme of late.

"I wish to heaven one of you three would settle down."

"One of us will, when the time's right."

"The time better turn right soon. I'm damned if

I'm going to die before I see the next generation of Wentworths get a toehold in this world.''

"You're too ornery to die even then. You'll stick around to make sure the kid learns how to suck oil from solid rock, like you did me.''

"I'd surely like to try," his grandfather replied, "if only one of you would get on with the business of marriage and baby making.''

It was a familiar refrain, one that Jack and his sister and brother had grown used to hearing. Josie merely laughed and kept her string of admirers dangling. Michael headed for Europe or the Caribbean with his latest amour whenever the old man started in on him again. And Jack...

Jack's standard reply was that he hadn't yet found a woman willing to take him, warts and all. Only he knew that he refused to allow any woman to get close to him. He couldn't. Hadn't wanted to.

Until Sabrina.

The thought was like a right cross to the chin. Instinctively, Jack wanted to duck, to spin away from the impact. Under Joseph's watchful eye, he maintained his comfortable sprawl, but his blood hammered another, more urgent message to his brain. The same message it had been pounding since he'd watched Sabrina drive away from him tonight.

He wanted to get more than close to her. He wanted her in his arms, her mouth fused with his. He wanted to feel her flush with heat, see her face come alive with laughter. He wanted her—

Hell, he wanted her.

It was as simple as that.

And as complicated.

He pushed himself to his feet, his hard-won calm shredded by the fiery need that licked at his veins once again.

"I'll see you tomorrow."

He gave his grandfather's shoulder an affectionate squeeze. The hand that came up to cover his was gnarled and liver-spotted, but returned the squeeze with barbed-wire strength.

"I'd rather you go see that woman you're so shut-mouthed about," Joseph said gruffly.

"I'm thinking about it."

The admission came hard. Slow. But when he said the words, damned if they didn't feel right.

The old man's shrewd brown eyes flared with interest, but he knew better than to dig too deep where Jack didn't want dug. Still, he couldn't let it go.

"You've always been restless, boy. Too loose-footed to stay put. Too ready to take off for the next sink or exploratory drill. This woman might be the one who'll anchor you as fast and as hard as a deep-sea rig."

She might at that.

The thought crawled up Jack's chest and into his heart as he strode down the black-and-white tiled corridor to his room. High, vaulted ceilings caught his footsteps and sent the echoes back down at him. Tugging at his tie, he tossed it aside as soon as he entered the two-room suite that had been his sanctuary as a boy. Now more of an office than a bedroom, its dark paneling, marble fireplace and tall, diamond-paned windows still held memories of youthful tussles with Mike and late-night visits by a wide-eyed, thumb-sucking Josie. Jack's suit coat followed the tie onto the back of a chair.

His body taut, he stripped and headed straight for the shower. The stinging needles that pelted down on his head and shoulders cleared his mind but did little for the smoldering fire deep in his gut. He went to bed recognizing that he had two choices.

He could travel down the road his gnawing need for Sabrina pointed him toward.

Or he could shut the tantalizing woman out of his mind once and for all.

It turned out to be no choice at all. Jack spent most of the night in a sweat, seeing images of shimmering green eyes and a full mouth swollen from his kiss. He dropped into sleep near dawn, and woke to the realization that he'd passed the point of having any choice at all the first time he'd taken Sabrina in his arms.

He strode into his Tulsa office atop the Wentworth Building just before seven. Sabrina had said she had an early class this morning. Fine. Jack intended to claim her afternoon...and whatever else she'd give him.

His executive assistant, of course, was already at his desk.

"I need you to clear my schedule from noon on," Jack instructed.

Pete Hastings didn't blink an eye. Tall, thin and impeccably dressed in a navy blazer and tan slacks, the former street bum understood that flexibility ranked at the top of the list of requirements for his job.

"No problem." Notepad and pen in hand, he followed his boss into the inner office. "Anything else?"

"Yes. I need the telephone number of the owner of the leases I looked at yesterday."

"It's in the file on your desk."

While Jack poured a cup of dark, rich coffee from the carafe already waiting for him, Pete pulled a neatly labeled folder from a brass tray.

"This is it."

"Thanks. Just leave it on the desk."

Setting the folder aside, the efficient assistant shuffled through the rest of the stack. He extracted two additional files, which joined the lease file on the desk.

"That's the final accident report from Fleet Operations on the Alaskan oil spill. You need to sign off on it so we can fax a copy to EPA. And I know you wanted to review this financial analysis before the meeting with Anderson Steel this morning. Everything else can wait."

"Good."

"Oh, what about this one?" Pete pulled a thin manila folder from the bottom of the stack. "It's the file on Sabrina Jensen, with the detailed financial data I requested. The information came in while you were in Alaska."

"I'll take it."

"The report doesn't contain anything significant," Pete advised.

"If it had," Jack replied with a smile as he skimmed the two pages, "you would have faxed it to me."

"You're right, of course." His assistant took the implied compliment in stride. "Financially, Ms. Jensen is stretched as thin as a wire, but she's kept herself out of debt and has an excellent credit rating. The small business loan she's applied for should sail through."

Unlocking his desk drawer, Jack dropped the file inside. "Take care of it, Pete."

"Considering that our bank is handling the transaction, that shouldn't be a problem."

"I didn't think so."

As soon as Pete cleared the office, Jack reached for the phone. He'd told Sabrina last night that he'd get her the name and the phone number of the man who owned the leases. He knew she wanted to arrange a salvage expedition to the old, tumble-down motel on the property. Jack now intended to do one better. He'd take her out to poke around the ruins himself.

And in the process, he'd take the next step down the path that beckoned brighter and surer with each passing hour. An absolute sense of rightness settled over him as he reached for the phone.

"Sure," the lease owner replied when Jack explained the reason for his call. "Your friend is welcome to anything she can salvage. She'd better get out there today, though," he warned. "After we shook on the deal yesterday afternoon, I lined up a crew to bulldoze the place. They're going in tomorrow."

"Can you hold them off if you have to?"

"It'll cost you."

"I figured it would," Jack replied dryly. "I'm hoping to get out there this afternoon, though."

His warning that Sabrina would insist on paying whatever she thought her finds were worth brought a chuckle.

"Fine by me. I'll sharpen my negotiating skills."

"You'd better. She knows what she's talking about when it comes to that era."

"She can't drive a harder bargain than you did," the owner drawled. "Hell, I'm still trying to figure out how I practically promised to pay *you* to take my leases."

Laughing, Jack assured him that they'd both come out winners on that deal. He hung up, wondering how he was going to get through the rest of the morning.

It was tough. Impatience to be away bit at him. As a result, Jack presided over the marathon, back-to-back meetings Pete had compressed into the next few hours with something less than his usual attention to detail. He barely waited until the door slammed behind the last group before he spun on his heel and headed for his private bathroom. He emerged mere moments later, tucking the tails of his white shirt into his jeans. Grabbing his straw Resistol, he made for the door.

He spent the drive out to the diner thinking of Sabrina as he'd last seen her, wide-eyed and flushed, her mouth swollen from his kiss.

Flushed and close to panting from the heat in the kitchen, Sabrina backed through the swinging door. Her knees cracked as she crouched to slide a heavy rack of clean mugs under the counter. Straightening, she arched her back to ease the ache the rack had caused and surveyed the crowded café.

One-thirty, and the lunch crowd had barely started to thin. The cash register had been pinging steadily for the past two hours. They'd run out of Hank's meat loaf special just past noon, and were now almost out of pie.

Not bad for a Wednesday. Not bad at all.

If only her nerves would stop bubbling and boiling like the fresh pot of chili Hank had just put on, she might take some satisfaction from the full register and her aching feet. She might not jump every time the front door opened. She might even stop expecting to see Jack Wentworth walk in.

He'd made it plain enough at the Petroleum Club last night what he wanted from her. Hot, mindless sex.

Okay. All right. Sabrina wanted the same thing. So bad her knees shook every time she remembered the feel of his mouth on hers. But during that sixteen-story plunge, she'd discovered that she also wanted more.

Like his arms around her for more than just a night.

Like a commitment he wasn't ready to give, a commitment she'd wasn't sure she wanted until that damned elevator ride.

Oh, Lord. Why didn't she just admit it? She wanted Jack Wentworth. With every breath she took. She'd gone to bed aching for him last night, and woken up to the same vicious ache. She'd driven to Stillwater in a daze, hadn't taken a single note in class. All morning long, desire had sizzled just below the surface of her skin, hot, urgent, a woman's need she no longer tried to deny. It rose up now, almost suffocating her with its heat.

She leaned against the counter, hands flat on the gray Formica, her stomach clenching. The noisy sounds and lively scents filling the air faded. She saw Jack, only Jack, his palms planted on either side of her in that tiny elevator, his blue eyes locked with hers, his mouth—

"Hey, Sabrina! Where's that chocolate pie?"

Reality came down with a thump.

"It's coming, it's coming!"

Hastily, she pulled an almost empty tin out of the refrigerated display case. She'd just picked up a spatula and started to slide it under the last wedge when the front door opened. The man who'd kept her tossing and turning for most of last night walked into the diner—tall, wide-shouldered and so darned handsome that the spatula slipped and her hand plunged deep into gooey chocolate.

Jack strolled up to the counter, his blue eyes glinting as he took in her predicament. "Hello, Sabrina. I hope that's not the last of the chocolate pie."

"Hey!" The burly-chested trucker seated at the counter growled out a protest. "That piece is spoken for."

Red-faced and more than a little dazed by the joy that danced in her chest, Sabrina wiped her gooey hand on the apron wrapped around her waist.

"I'm sorry, Dave. Looks like I did a number on this piece. How about some carrot cake? I promise I won't put my paw through that."

Her rueful smile raised a tide of red on the trucker's neck. "Aw, hell, Sabrina, a little rearrangin' don't matter to me. Just scoop the remains onto a plate and shove 'em my way."

The fact that she did just that said volumes about her state of mind. While Dave attacked his mangled dessert, Sabrina tried to catch her breath, and failed. Still dazed, still breathless, she smiled at Jack.

"What are you doing here?"

"I promised last night that I'd put you in touch

with the owner of that old motel that's going to be torn down, remember?''

Silly question. She remembered *everything* about last night, including how close she'd come to melting into a puddle of need in this man's arms.

"I called him this morning, and it's a good thing that I did. He's already got a demolition crew lined up for tomorrow. We need to get out there this afternoon to beat the bulldozers.''

"This afternoon!'' Dismayed, Sabrina glanced around the busy diner. "I can't this afternoon.''

"Sure you can.'' Peg strolled up, her dark eyes smiling. "I'll take care of these boys. You go take care of yours.''

Sabrina didn't dispute the claim. With everyone in the diner observing the almost visible sparks that arced between her and Jack, she knew it was hopeless even to try. Heat stained her cheeks as she made a last check.

"Are you sure you can manage?''

"Honey, I was slinging plates and pouring Hank's undrinkable coffee before you were born. Go on, get out of here.''

"Thanks. I'll be back as soon as I can.''

Peg's gaze slewed to Jack. "Take your time,'' she drawled.

Her face redder than ever, Sabrina pushed through the door to tell Hank about her expedition and snatch her purse from the desk in the little office at the rear of the diner. Wishing fervently she had a clean shirt to change into, she dragged a brush through her hair and sneaked a quick spritz of Rachel's Christmas gift to her. White Diamonds and Hank's meat loaf, she thought ruefully. If that combination didn't get to a man, nothing would.

It definitely got to Jack.

They'd no sooner crossed the parking lot to the red Wentworth truck than he spun her around. His hands were rough and urgent. His mouth even more so.

Sabrina's pulse stopped dead, then took off like a thoroughbred just out of the chute. Her knees almost folding under her, she dug her fingers into Jack's upper arms for balance, for support, for the sheer jolt that touching him gave her.

The dusty, sun-heated parking lot was spinning when he dragged his head up. Sabrina held on, waiting for the universe to right itself. Jack recovered long before she did, although there was a ragged edge to the smile that started at a corner of his mouth and creased one tanned cheek.

"Damn! I swore I wouldn't do that."

"Why not?" she croaked.

Groaning, he rested his forehead against hers. "Because I was afraid that once I started, even those bulldozers couldn't stop me."

Sabrina started to tell him that she didn't want him to stop, not now, not ever, but he was already pulling away from her.

"Let's get out to this motel," he said with a savage

note in his voice that thrilled her to the tips of her toes. ''Then we have to talk.''

Talk was good, she decided. Talk meant he had something on his mind other than meaningless sex. Now if only she could think of something, anything, else herself!

Her heart knocking, she climbed into the red truck with the Wentworth Oil logo on the side panel. In that bright, sunlit moment, with the dust rising in lazy swirls and bees humming through the alfalfa fields around the diner, Sabrina couldn't know that she and Jack would never have their promised talk...or that she'd barely survive the visit to the dilapidated ruin that had once provided only shelter and comfort.

Chapter 9

The accident happened so swiftly, so unexpectedly, that Sabrina hardly knew what hit her.

Afterward, she would remember waiting impatiently while Jack dug a toolbox out of the truck. She'd also remember following the broken chunks of concrete that once formed a stretch of the original Route 66. She could almost smell the rich aromas of hot, verdant earth, of old asphalt baking in the sun, of the wild honeysuckle that clung and curved and twisted in riotous glory along what was once a neat picket fence. And she would certainly recall Jack's insistence that he go first, since he was wearing tough leather boots, which would provide more protection than her sneakers against any snakes they might disturb.

Most of all, Sabrina would remember her first glimpse of the Sleep Well Motor Court. When the cluster of ramshackle structures came into view, she stopped in her tracks, enchanted.

"Oh, Jack, look at that well!"

The handcrafted, shingle-topped wishing well that must have given the place its name tipped drunkenly in the center of the weed-grown yard.

"I bet every kid who stayed here begged a penny from their parents to toss into that little well."

Jack grinned. "No doubt that was what the management had in mind."

"No doubt," Sabrina agreed, laughing. "But I'd like to think some of the folks who traveled the Mother Road got their wishes at the end of it."

Eagerly, she eyed the dozen or so cabins that hunkered in a semicircle behind the well. Shaded by pungent, orange-flowering mimosa trees, the one-room structures were now almost uniformly gray, although faint traces of the original white paint and green trim showed here and there. Most of the roofs had collapsed inward. Broken windows stared sightlessly at the sun. Despite the motor court's sorry condition, Sabrina had no difficulty picturing the place as it once was.

Fan-shaped iron chairs much like the one she lazed in during her breaks at the diner would have dotted the porches. Pictures cut from the glossy magazines of the day would have decorated the walls. She could almost see the chenille bedspreads, smell the damp and mildew in cold, dreary Januaries, hear the ancient plumbing groan when the toilets flushed.

Families would have stopped here, she mused, crowding into a single cabin to save on expenses. Businessmen traveling America's most famous highway no doubt parked their huge Hudsons or DeSotos in front of those green-painted doors. Lovers slipping away for a stolen night sank into sagging mattresses.

Sabrina had a good idea of the laughter these old walls would have absorbed, the tired sighs, the tears, the muffled groans. She and Rachel had spent more nights than she could count in modern-day versions of this old motor court. Her father still called them home, when he didn't just pull over and sleep in his truck cab.

That impermanence was part of Sabrina's past... but not her future, she reminded herself. Her dreams were built on the lure of the old road, but they were grounded in the red dirt of Oklahoma. Or more specifically, in the diner planted atop that red dirt.

She eyed the crumbling ruins, eager to get on with her explorations. "The owner said we could salvage whatever we wanted, right?"

"Right. And anything we can't haul away today, he'll have the demolition crew pull out before they raze the place tomorrow. He warned me that there isn't much here except cobwebs and rusty pipes, though. This hunting expedition might be a total bust, Sabrina."

"Maybe. Maybe not. Let's find out."

She started toward the end unit. Jack caught her with a firm hand on her arm.

"I'll go first."

Seriously hoping that they didn't encounter anything more annoying than the gnats that swarmed around her with each step, Sabrina followed him up the weed-clogged gravel drive to the cabin at the far end of the semicircle. She bit her lip nervously when he tested his weight on the rotting floorboards of the porch, then shouldered aside a door hanging by only one hinge.

"Watch out for bees," he warned as she stepped around him. "They like to hive in ruins like these."

She poked around cautiously. Aside from hanging strips of water-splotched flowered wallpaper and a rusted floor heater with broken elements, she found few traces of a bygone era.

The roof of the next cabin had remained more or less intact, but the floorboards were so warped and rotted that Jack refused to trust them with his weight or hers.

By the time they'd checked out the third and fourth cabins, Sabrina was beginning to doubt she'd find anything worth scavenging. To her delight, they hit pay dirt in the fifth. Under a fold of sagging wallboard, she spotted some iron light fixtures. Their etched glass shades were miraculously intact.

"Jack, look! Wouldn't those look perfect mounted on either side of the jukebox."

"You'll have to have them rewired."

"No problem. I know an electrician who'll take care of that in exchange for a free meal."

Under her anxious direction, Jack propped up the wall and wrestled the fixtures loose. Sabrina wrapped them in the newspaper they'd brought along for just that purpose and happily tucked them in a cardboard box.

In the seventh cabin, Jack found some moldy, tattered *Look* magazines. She snatched them up in the fervent hope that some of the pages had survived the ravages of time. To her delight, she found colorful advertisements and fifties-era stories perfect for framing.

In the tenth, they discovered the remains of a bedroom set. Rot had eaten away most of its blond veneer and art deco styling, but Sabrina was sure she could restore the dressing table to its original glory.

"That's perfect for the ladies' room at the diner," she declared. "I know where I can get a mirror to match!"

Obligingly, Jack carted the piece out to the truck.

But it was the office that yielded the real treasure. Only a little larger than the other structures, its wooden counter had long since crumbled into dust. Sunlight slanted through its collapsed roof. Vines crawled over the sills of the broken windows and all but covered the walls. Sabrina poked and peered and carefully pried up a fallen board or two. She found nothing to excite her until she turned, ready to leave. The glint of sunlight on something shiny caught her almost at the door. Squatting to see under the fallen roof, she spied the cracked glass of a framed advertisement for Phillips 66 gasoline.

The poster was done in black and white. Time had given it a patina of yellow, but hadn't diminished the sultry beauty of the platinum blonde with charcoaled eyes, pouty lips, and geometrically precise spit curls. She had turned her back on an art deco outline of Chicago and fixed her gaze firmly on the dazzling rainbow of California at the end of the road. The faded print underneath proclaimed that even the stars got their kicks on Route 66. And, if that faint scrawl across the bottom wasn't dirt or a water stain, the print was signed!

Sabrina gave a gasp of pure delight. Reaching up, she grabbed a fistful of Jack's shirt and dragged him into a crouch beside her.

"That's Jean Harlow! I'm sure of it." She swiveled on her heels. "Maybe she stayed here once and signed the poster for the owner."

The sparkling excitement on her face had Jack grinning. Despite the dirt, the gnats and the stink of rot, Sabrina was in heaven. He had to admit he wasn't far from it himself. He couldn't remember a ramble through the past that had given him as much pleasure as this one…or a woman who torched his senses like Sabrina did. Cobwebs coated her hair. A streak of dirt ran across one cheek. Her tank top and jeans were as dusty as his, and he was sure he'd never seen anything as vibrant, as vital, as this woman.

"I have to have that print!"

Laughing at her unabashed greed, he pushed off his heels. "Let me find something to shore up the roof first."

He'd taken only a step, maybe two, when Sabrina shrieked. Jack spun around just in time to see the rusted pipe she'd grasped to pull herself upright come clattering down. The rest of the sagging roof came with it.

She flung up her arms to protect her head at the exact instant Jack launched himself through the falling debris. He took her down, covering her body with his as a crashing torrent of rotting timbers, crumbling plaster and tar paper buried them both.

His muscles flinched at each blow. His nostrils filling with dust and fine, white granules of plaster, he dug his fists into Sabrina's hair, jerking her head into his shoulder as a chunk of ceiling crashed down mere inches away. Through the groan and shriek of tearing timbers he cursed himself viciously for ever mentioning the damned motor court to Sabrina, for not taking the precaution of having the ceilings shored up before he brought her here, for letting his woman walk right into a crumbling ruin.

Finally, the raining debris slowed to a trickle, then to sporadic spills. Nose and throat filled with dust, he levered one shoulder against the crushing weight.

"Sabrina!"

Her eyes were closed, her face coated a deathly

white. Jack's gut twisted. Panic roughened his voice and his hands still fisted in her hair.

"Sabrina, are you all right?"

She lifted one lid, groaned, closed it again.

"I...can't...breathe."

Jack had been in some tight spots in his time. The summer after his junior year in college, he and the drilling crew he'd been working with had been caught by a racing, wind-whipped prairie fire. They'd plunged to the safety of a river through smoke and scorching heat scant inches ahead of the roaring flames.

Once, during his stint with the SEABEEs, an underwater demolition charge had gone off in one of his men's hands, killing the sailor and injuring two others. Face mask shattered and scuba tank pumping air bubbles into the dark, silent sea, Jack had dragged the wounded men to the surface.

Years later, he'd stood beside Ali in the deserts of Qatar to fight off a vicious, bloody attack by El Jafir.

But never, ever, in those desperate situations had Jack felt anything like the fear that riffled through him now. Throat tight, panic seeping from every one of his pores, he pushed himself up a few more inches.

"Sabrina. Sweetheart. Tell me where you hurt."

"My...stomach." Her eyes fluttered open. "Your knee...is...digging a hole in...it."

The icy fear in Jack's veins melted in a hot, sweet rush. Half laughing, half groaning, he shifted. The small movement caused another shower of plaster and an ominous creak right above his head. He froze, waited for the dust to settle, then tried again more cautiously.

It took him a good ten minutes to wiggle, push, grunt and shove free. Finally, the heaviest timber tumbled off his back. Jack got a knee, then a boot, under him. Sliding his arms under Sabrina, he scooped her from her dusty cradle.

Blinding light engulfed them the instant they stepped outside the cabin. Not about to risk a fall, Jack waited until his eyes had adjusted to the blazing light before starting for the truck. Sabrina blew upward to clear the dust from her face.

"I...I can walk."

"Maybe." Jack tightened his hold. "But I can't let you go."

Her eyes widened at that, but she didn't argue. Her arm curled around his neck. Her breath fanned his ear, as erratic and uneven as his. Jack could feel her heart punching against her ribs. His own was doing exactly the same.

By the time he spotted the truck, his blood thundered in his ears almost as loudly as the falling timbers had. Sabrina's rounded bottom nudged his stomach with every step. The hot wash of her breath was driving fear, relief, even fury at his own stupidity for putting her in danger right out of his head.

Wrenching open the passenger door, Jack eased her onto the passenger seat. His stomach kicked again at her dusty pallor.

"Hang tight. There's some bottled water in the back."

Water and a first aid kit. He retrieved both and set to work. Worried about possible scratches and puncture wounds from the rusty pipe or roofing nails, he cleaned her face, her hands, her arms, then checked her stretchy knit shirt front and back for rips and tears.

Aside from a nasty scrape on one elbow and a rising lump on her collarbone, Sabrina had come through the near disaster remarkably unscathed. She winced when Jack smoothed a stinging antiseptic ointment on her scrape, then took the tube out of his hands.

"You took more of the avalanche than I did. Your shirt's torn at the shoulders. You'd better take it off and let me put some ointment on your cuts and scrapes."

When he shrugged out of the once pristine white shirt and turned, Sabrina had to bite back a gasp. Angry red welts scored his skin. An evil bruise had already started forming along his ribs. Spreading her legs to cradle his hips, she squeezed a big dollop of ointment into either palm.

If she'd thought about it at that moment, Sabrina would have sworn that few experiences in life could match the heart-stopping impact of having a building fall in on her.

Then her flesh connected with Jack's.

Her touch was slow, soft, light on the sore spots. Her fingertips trailed lightly across muscled shoulders. Down a well-defined spine. Along a jagged scar that traced the curve of a rib. He was, she decided, magnificent.

The greasy ointment made her movements a slow glide of discovery, a stroke, a caress. His skin was warm and supple under her fingers. With each stroke, each joining of her flesh to his, the need that had been building since the moment she'd opened her eyes and found Jack smiling down at her ripened, blossomed, opened like a flower unfolding its petals to the sun. Sabrina couldn't speak for wanting him. Could barely breathe.

Suddenly, his skin rippled under her palms, and she heard a low, raw sound. To her surprise, Sabrina realized it came from her.

Jack caught the small groan and whipped around. He was so big he blocked the rest of the world from view, so close she could see the dust in the brows that slashed into a tight, worried frown.

"Are you sure you're all right?"

"No." She bit her lip, dragged in an unsteady breath. "I think I'm in shock."

Cursing, he bent to scoop up his shirt. "I'd better get you into town."

"Jack, it's not that kind of—"

"I must have been out of my mind to bring you out here."

Shoving one arm into his shirt, he fought behind his back for the other sleeve.

"Jack…"

"Don't try to talk! Just put your head back. Stay still while I—"

She cut off his whip of instructions by the simple expedient of wrapping both arms around his neck, hauling him down, and crushing her mouth to his.

He stumbled into her, off balance, his arms still tangled in the sleeves behind his back. She took his weight on her breasts, her spread thighs. The sudden, erotic press against the seam of her jeans sent a lightning bolt of pure sensation straight to her brain.

She pulled her head back, smiling at the stunned look in his eyes.

"It's not that kind of shock." She brushed her mouth against his once more. "It's this kind." Her tongue slid along his lower lip. "And this kind."

"Sabrina! Dammit..."

"And this kind, Jack."

Her arms tightened. She raised half off the seat, molded her mouth to his once more, gloried in his dark, seductive taste.

He froze. For what seemed like a small eternity, he didn't answer the urgent demand of Sabrina's mouth and hands and body. Then, suddenly, his muscles bunched. Swearing, straining, smothering her with the heat that rose in waves from his body, he finally wrenched one arm free of his shirt. A heartbeat later, he buried his hands in her hair and tugged her head back.

"Sabrina, listen to me. I want you. I've wanted you since the first moment I saw you lazing like a cat behind the diner. If you kiss me like that again, I swear I'll have your clothes off before you draw another breath.''

It was a threat. A promise. A low, savage vow.

Back bent, neck arched, scalp tingling where his grip tugged at her hair, she flashed him a grin.

''So, what's the problem?''

He groaned. A vein popped out on his forehead. Barely able to breathe for the heat curling through her body, Sabrina stared up at him.

''The problem is what we talked about last night. We were worried about getting in too fast and too deep. I'm not worried anymore, but you...?''

''I'm still nervous,'' she admitted with bruising honesty. ''We're from different worlds. We have different needs, different dreams. But if you don't make love to me in the next sixty seconds, I think...no, I'm pretty sure...I'll die.''

Jack groaned again. Or maybe he snarled. Since his hands and his mouth were all over her, Sabrina couldn't tell which. Her stretchy knit top ripped over her head. The waistband of her jeans popped open. He lifted her up, then dropped her back on the vinyl truck seat a few seconds later minus jeans, minus panties, minus breath.

As before, her thighs spread to accommodate him. As before, the hard, driving pressure against her mound sent streaks of pure sensation straight to her brain. She almost sobbed with pleasure when Jack shaped her breast.

His hands both rough and gentle, he worried the aching nipple. It went rigid at his touch, his taste, his tender-sharp kisses. Sabrina arched back, her hands flat on the seat behind her, glorying in his need. Her own hunger soon fired too hot to let her take and not give. The fingers that had skimmed so lightly over his back dug into his shoulders. She explored his contours, his strength, his slick, hot skin with the same urgency, the same racing delight as he'd explored hers.

She was spinning on a spiral of white-hot sensation when he stepped back.

"Jack..."

"I don't want to run over my sixty seconds, sweetheart, but I need to—"

"I'll help," Sabrina panted, fumbling with the snap on his jeans.

A moment later, he was jutting, magnificent. Sliding an arm around Sabrina's waist, he dragged her forward, half off the seat and hard against him. His fingers parted her folds, probed her slick center. With a deliberation that drove her half out of her mind, he primed her, pumped her, soon had her sobbing.

Through it all, her mouth and her hands and her heart gloried in the feel of his.

At last he entered her. He stretched her, filled her, and soon built a wild rhythm. Up, down, up, down, like a well-lubricated oil rig lifting, plunging, pulling treasures from the hidden depths.

Jack felt the jagged, saw-toothed edge of his release

long before he was ready. He gritted his teeth, determined to hold back, to push Sabrina to her peak before he blew. The effort beaded sweat on his arms and chest, already slick from the friction of her body against his.

Wedging his back against the door frame, he dug his hands into her waist, anchored her, and thrust upward. Her back arched, and he thrust again.

"Jack! I can't...! I don't...!"

"You don't have to, Sabrina. Just let go."

She flung her head back. A long, ragged groan tore from her throat. He felt her convulse around him, tight and hot and long.

Jack held himself rigid while she climaxed, his every muscle on fire with the strain. He'd never seen anything so beautiful, he thought savagely. So wild. So damned incredible. Then he began his own swift, searing climb to the sun.

It took some time for Sabrina to realize that the buzzing in her ears came not from her explosive climax, but from the pesky little gnats that had flitted into the truck. She opened her eyes, lifted a boneless arm, and swatted them away. In the process, she drew a rueful smile from Jack.

"I fantasized about this moment." His voice was rough and achingly tender.

"Me, too."

He used his hold on her waist to lift her more comfortably onto the truck seat. If Sabrina hadn't been totally boneless and drained of every ounce of energy, she might have marveled that her nakedness didn't embarrass her. As it was, she could only sigh in pleasure while he traced a line along her cheek with his knuckles.

"I know I talked about a couple of hours of hot, mindless sex, but I didn't intend..." he glanced around the overgrown, sun-dappled road "...this."

"Do you hear me complaining?"

He brushed back her hair. "I had planned soft lights, cool sheets and a slow, sweet seduction. I wanted the best for you, sweetheart."

She saw that he was serious, that he thought she needed more. He didn't realize how magnificent he was. How just the sight of his dust-coated brown hair and sweat-sheened shoulders glinting in the hot sun was making her crazy all over again. Smiling, she turned her head and planted a kiss on his knuckles.

"Much as I hate to pander to your ego, Mr. Wentworth, I think...no, I'm almost sure—I just had the best."

One dusty brow hitched. "Almost, huh?"

"Well, I might need another sample or two or three to make sure."

"That, Ms. Jensen, can be arranged."

Suddenly, disconcertingly brisk, he scooped up their scattered clothing.

"Here, you get dressed while I see if your poster survived the crash."

"No!" She grabbed at his arm as he stepped into

his jeans. "Don't go back in there. I couldn't take another roof falling in on you in one day."

"I'll be careful." He dropped a quick kiss on her nose. "Just get dressed, then we'll head back to your place. It's closer. You can use the phone in the truck to call Hank and let him know you won't be back to work today."

He strode off, and Sabrina's rosy glow dimmed a bit around the edges. Obviously Jack was used to taking charge and making decisions.

So was she.

She couldn't think of anything she'd rather do at this moment than tumble out of a shower onto cool sheets with this fascinating, irresistibly sexy man. But she couldn't go weak at the knees and fall into his arms every time he smiled at her, or walk away from her job on a whim. She might not chair a multinational corporation, but she, too, had certain responsibilities.

By the time Jack returned with the poster, Sabrina had pulled on her top and jeans. He stowed the salvaged items in the truck bed, then slid behind the wheel.

"Jean Harlow took a few hits, but a good restorer should be able to get her back in star condition."

"That's okay. I'm just glad all three of us survived."

"Ready?"

Nodding, she propped one sneaker on the seat to tie the laces.

He keyed the ignition and wrapped his hand around the gearshift. ''Did you get hold of Hank?''

''I didn't try.''

He shot her a quick look. Calmly, Sabrina hiked up her other foot.

''I can't take the rest of the day off.'' She softened the blunt statement with a swift, sideways smile. ''I wish I could. Believe me, I wish I could. But Peg has to take her daughter to the dentist at four-thirty and the part-timer doesn't come on until five.''

Her foot dropped to the floorboard.

Jack couldn't miss the message in that solid whump. Or in those clear green eyes. Obviously, he'd run smack up against Sabrina's stubborn independence and pride again. He admired both. Nor could he fault the sense of responsibility that pushed her back to work, even if the prospect of a wait raised a clamoring protest. His nerves sang with the need to taste her again, to fill her again, and again. Swallowing an impatience so sharp, so alive, it ate at him, he shoved the truck into gear.

''Okay. We'll go back to your place. We'll clean up, and we'll take you back to work. After work, we'll see about giving you that sample or two or three.''

Sabrina didn't get back to work that afternoon.

She started feeling drowsy on the way home. It could have been the hum of the tires that lulled her. Or the fact that she'd hit the ground running before five this morning. Or the fact that a roof had fallen in on her twice today, once in the old motor court, once in Jack's arms.

At any rate, she was content to listen to the soothing resonance of his voice on the drive home and watch the mesmerizing wink of sunshine through the trees. She was half asleep when the truck turned into her driveway and she led the way inside the house, offering Jack first dibs on the bathroom.

She was sound asleep when he stepped out of her tiny shower fifteen minutes later.

Jack hooked his hands on the towel slung around his neck, his mouth curving. She was curled in a loose ball in the middle of the bed. She'd shucked her sneakers and dirty jeans, but little else. Sighing, he considered his options.

He'd cleared his calendar for the rest of the day.

Sabrina hadn't.

He could wake her and drive her back to work.

Or let her sleep.

With a last, regretful glance at her tucked-up legs and curved bottom, he returned the towel to the tiny bathroom and buttoned his borrowed shirt.

Chapter 10

Sabrina came out of a dreamless sleep to a room filled with warm, summer sun. Stretching, she let her gaze drift with sleepy curiosity to the alarm clock beside the bed.

Her eyes widened. No way! It couldn't possibly be six-forty! She blinked, shot a look at the window, and gasped at the slanting rays that cut at a sharp angle across the room.

Disbelief rattled into dismay. She rolled upright in the bed, frowning at the pull of a sore muscle. Her hand went to the small of her back as the sharp ache pierced her lingering grogginess. Like a kaleidoscope, fractured images clicked into place in her mind. The motor court. The falling roof. The man who'd pulled her from under the debris and made fierce, wicked love with her.

Her stomach hollowed as the images rolled on. The hot sun. The endless blue sky. Jack's sweat-slicked body locked with hers.

Jack!

Her heart thumping, Sabrina listened for some sounds of his presence. All she heard was a faint drip from the shower.

"Jack?"

Flustered by the late hour and the silence, she pushed off the bed. It took only a moment or two to ascertain that he had left. Sabrina stood in the living room, staring at the salvaged light fixtures, the shabby dressing table, and the dented poster of Jean Harlowe that Jack had stacked just inside her front door. Clenching her fists, she fought bitter waves of disappointment.

"Don't be stupid," she muttered fiercely, spinning around to head back to the bedroom. "The man has a corporation to run. A home to go back to."

And a busy, jet-set life that didn't include her.

Still, a goodbye would have been nice, or so she informed the dust-streaked face that frowned back at her from the bathroom mirror.

A goodbye and an indication, however casual, that he wanted to see her again.

More hurt than she was willing to admit, Sabrina set about removing all traces of the afternoon's tumultuous events. Ten minutes later, she rushed through the kitchen and slammed the door shut behind her. The few miles to the diner sped by while Sabrina reminded herself that neither she nor Jack had made any promises, that what happened was as much her doing as his. She'd practically attacked the man this afternoon.

Sighing, she whipped into the diner's still-crowded parking lot. Guilt at having left Hank and Peg in a lurch during the supper rush had her skimming her Mazda into a convenient space between two eighteen-wheelers instead of weaving around to her usual spot in the rear lot.

She hurried up the steps and through the front door. With a smile to a few of her regulars, she wove through the noisy crowd. She spotted her boss peering through the backlog of orders stacked up on the pass-through from the kitchen.

"Hi, Hank. I'm so sorry! I didn't mean to be gone this long."

He gummed his cigar from one corner of his mouth to the other. "We managed, although I'm sure glad that sub who came in to cover for you doesn't have to make a living waiting tables."

Thinking he referred to the high schooler who worked part-time, Sabrina winced. "She couldn't handle the crowd, huh?"

"Oh, the crowd's not the problem. It's..."

The sound of a plate smashing onto the tile floor had them both flinching.

"It's that," Hank finished dryly.

"I'm sorry," she said again. Stashing her purse under the counter, she grabbed a broom and dustpan from behind the kitchen door. "I'll help get that cleaned up and start working those backed-up orders. Just give me…"

Sabrina took only a step, then stopped in her tracks. Her jaw sagging, she gaped at the apron-clad figure hunkered down beside one of the booths. Under the apron he wore one of her father's old denim work shirts that she had appropriated to study and sleep in. He must have filched it from her bedroom, she thought dazedly.

Jack glanced up then and caught her openmouthed stare. Grinning, he crossed an arm over his bent knee.

"I think I need a little more on-the-job training. Peg gave me a crash course before she left to take her daughter to the dentist, but I obviously missed some of the more subtle tricks of the trade. Like how the heck you maneuver two armloads of plates *off* your arms and *onto* the table."

"You get someone to help you," the giggling high schooler put in.

"Or you don't load up both arms," Hank drawled.

"Or you slide the plates onto the table, instead of bouncing 'em," the customer whose dinner had ended up on the floor contributed dryly.

"Slide, huh?" Jack pondered the technique, undisturbed by the snickers rising from the other booths. "I'll have to try that next time."

Sabrina finally found her voice. "What in the world are you doing here?"

His grin softened to a private smile. ''Letting Sleeping Beauty snatch a few more *Z*s.''

''But...? Why...?'' Flustered, she could only shake her head. ''You should have woken me.''

''I tried. When you sleep, Sabrina, you sleep.''

Suddenly mindful of their rapt audience, she flushed and dropped to one heel beside him. The broom swished up the broken plate and spilled food with brisk efficiency.

''You could've at least told me you were coming out to the diner,'' she murmured. ''I thought you'd driven back to Tulsa or wherever.''

''Didn't you read the note?''

''What note?''

''I left it propped on the kitchen table.''

''I didn't see it.''

She hadn't seen anything beyond her disappointment that Jack had left her. Now, she couldn't see anything beyond the smile that lightened his eyes. It made her heart start flashing and singing like the old Wurlitzer jukebox when one of the customers fed it quarters.

He hadn't left her. He'd let her sleep and come to fill in for her. Sabrina couldn't remember receiving a more generous gift from anyone. The need that had consumed her this afternoon deepened, softened, sweetened.

He must have seen it in her face, or in the smile she gave him in return for his unexpected gift. His voice dropped to a husky whisper in her ear.

"You're beautiful asleep, Sabrina."

"I'm awake now," she answered with a shiver of delight. "I'll take it from here."

She did. Effortlessly and flawlessly.

Watching from the stool he'd retired to, Jack decided that she could give a time-and-motion expert lessons. Measuring her performance by the yardstick of his own admittedly limited experience, he could only admire the way she served up a generous helping of laughter along with endless platters of chicken-fried steak, onion burgers and pecan pie.

Her hands were never empty, her feet never still. She carried coffeepots, silverware and full platters on the way to the crowded tables, empty plates and glasses on the way back. In between, she took orders, mixed salads, dished up desserts, manned the cash register and changed the soft drink dispensers.

Most of the clientele in the place obviously knew and liked Sabrina. Some, Jack discovered a half hour later, liked her a little too well. He nursed a cup of coffee and glowered at a particularly obnoxious jerk in the black T-shirt and bill-to-the-back yellow ball cap. The trucker had trundled his eighteen-wheeler into the parking lot with a roar that rattled the diner's windows and hadn't stopped making noise since. Sabrina returned his wisecracks handily enough, but the man was starting to get on Jack's nerves. The look in the trucker's bloodshot eyes as he held up his coffee cup didn't exactly improve matters.

"Hey, Sabrina, how about a refill?"

Busy collecting an order from the pass-through window, she called an answer over her shoulder. "I'll take care of you in a minute."

"Yeah, and I'd like to take care of you, too, baby doll."

The lascivious comment earned him scowls from the customers seated beside him. The little smacking noises he made when Sabrina bent over to snag a ketchup bottle from under the counter brought Jack right off his stool. Before he'd taken more than a single step around the counter, Sabrina straightened and shot him a look that told him to back off.

She handled the situation with a smile and a smooth style all her own. After delivering the order, she strolled to the end of the counter. The glass carafe in her hand steamed with scalding, fresh-brewed coffee.

"Do you want this in your cup or over your head?" she asked calmly.

"Huh?"

"The next time you make a rude noise or a comment like that, I won't ask."

She filled his cup, then hooked a hand on her hip and waited patiently. It took the cretin a while, but he finally figured out what she expected from him.

"I, uh, didn't mean anything."

She arched a brow, still waiting.

"Sorry, Sabrina."

"Apology accepted," she said easily. "How about

a piece of pie to go with your coffee? There's some
lemon meringue left.''

Jack settled back on his stool. The urge to violence
still ripped at him. He knew how to take care of himself, had participated in his share of brawls during his
rowdy youth, but he'd long since learned the value of
negotiation over brute force. Yet he would have
wiped the linoleum with the jackass at the other end
of the counter if the man hadn't apologized.

Almost as strong as the urge to violence was the
primal urge to mark his territory. To stake a claim.
Permanently. Irrevocably.

And he would. Later. When they were alone. When
they'd had a chance to talk. When he could tell her
about the decisions he'd come to last night, all of
which concerned her.

Jack flicked a glance at the clock over the counter.
Four more hours until the diner closed. Probably
closer to five until he could take Sabrina home, kiss
her senseless, tumble her into bed. Then talk.

It was, he realized, going to be a long night.

Finishing off his coffee, he decided to go out to
the truck to check in with his office, then the Wentworth operations center. That would kill a half hour
or so. Spinning erotic fantasies about what he intended to do with—and to—Sabrina later would kill
the rest.

Or kill him.

It was a close call.

Jack couldn't remember wanting more or aching

harder in his life. He was waiting beside the Mazda when Sabrina walked out of the diner into a night spangled with a couple of million stars and the sweet scent of new-mown grass. The arms she slid around his neck were warm and eager, her kiss as hungry as his. But her weary sigh when she settled against his chest neatly sabotaged his agenda for the rest of the night.

"Tired?"

"Yes. No." Laughter bubbled up. "Yes. It's been quite a day."

Jack didn't comment on the fact that he'd spent the past several hours thinking of ways to stretch the day even further into the night. Instead, he reached for her car keys.

"We can leave my truck here overnight. I'll drive your Mazda, and you just relax."

He'd just more or less announced that he wanted to spend the night in her bed, and she was supposed to relax? Sabrina didn't think so.

"I'm okay," she said a trifle breathlessly. "I'll drive my car and you can follow. It's only a few miles."

The truth, she admitted as she slid behind the wheel, was that she needed those few miles to get her fluttery nerves under control. She'd spent the whole blessed evening on a blade of anticipation, as conscious of Jack's presence in the diner as a tethered goat watched by a lazy mountain lion. His every movement feathered her nerves. His smile came close to causing her to put another hand into the pie. If that weren't bad enough, all she had to do was think about the rumpled bed waiting for them at home and her lungs squeezed painfully.

They were still squeezing when she pulled into the carport. The truck's lights flashed in the rearview mirror, blinding her for a moment. She squinched against the glare, then heard Jack's boots as they crunched on the drive. He held out a hand to help her out. The simple touch sparked white flashes of heat through her body.

She led him through the side door. Sure enough, a folded piece of white notebook paper was propped against the pile of textbooks on the kitchen table. She'd missed it completely.

"Would you like a drink? Rachel brought a bottle of wine with her a few weeks ago." Sabrina reached for the fridge handle. "Or there may be a bottle or two of beer left from Dad's last swing through."

Jack caught her arm. "Unless you want some, I'll pass. I swigged enough coffee while I watched you in action to keep me awake all night."

She cocked her head, her eyes wide and too innocent. "All night, huh?"

"All night," he repeated with a grin.

She gave a little groan, partly in response to the sheer male bravado in his boast and partly from the excitement that streaked through her when he bent his head.

His mouth covered hers. This kiss held everything they'd bypassed this afternoon. Tenderness. Slow, sensual exploration. Wonder.

All too soon, it escalated into greedy hunger. When Sabrina finally pulled back, her legs were as shaky as her breath.

"If you expect me to last longer than the next ten minutes, we'd better slow down these kisses."

"Honey, we're going to slow everything down."

The smile that accompanied that promise had her heart bumping even before he slid an arm under her knees and brought her to his chest. True to his word, he strolled down the hall and eased her onto the rumpled bed.

He loomed over her, his face a play of light and dark in the shadows. He slipped off her sneakers, and Sabrina's throat went dry when he unsnapped her jeans and slowly peeled them down her hips. Then he wrapped both hands around her foot. His skin was warm against hers. Excited and nervous and suddenly, ridiculously shy, she propped herself up on one elbow.

"What are you...? Oh, Jack! Oh! Oooh!"

She plopped back on the quilt, sure she would drown in a river of pleasure. His strong, sure hands worked magic on her aching arches, her toes, her heels. He massaged one foot, then the other. Each exertion, each pressure eased aches she hadn't even known she had.

"If you ever decide to retire from the oil-and-gas

business," Sabrina gasped between ripples of sheer pleasure, "you could make a fortune doing feet. Another fortune," she amended on a shuddering sigh.

"What makes you think feet are my only talent?"

His wonderful, magical fingers moved to her ankle. He rotated the joint, loosening it, then slid his palms along her calf. Kneading, knuckling, stroking, he had her quivering all over. Certain she'd died and gone to waitress heaven, Sabrina closed her eyes and gave herself up to the exquisite sensation.

Afterward, she was never quite sure when she first realized that her legs were untapped, unmapped erogenous zones. Maybe when the pleasure shifted from joyous little spurts to slow, decadent streams. Or when Jack's fingers found an aching knot of muscle just above her knees. She jerked. Murmuring an apology, he laid a kiss on the tender area.

She jerked again at the hot touch of his tongue. And again, when he edged her panties down and trailed kisses across her hips, her belly. He bared her breasts, her throat. She was swimming in fire by the time his skilled mouth finally reached hers.

"Now you, Jack," she panted what seemed like hours later. "Let me see you. Let me pleasure you."

"Slowly," he reminded, his voice rough, tender, a little hoarse.

"Slowly," she promised, hers liquid with desire.

He heeled off his boots, and Sabrina took over from there. Rising up on her knees, she unbuttoned his borrowed shirt. Her mouth was as soft as a cloud on the

dark bruise that crept across one shoulder. Her hands
were gentle on his back.

Despite her butterfly touch, or maybe because of it,
his skin rippled under her fingers like a fast-moving
stream. His neck corded under her lips. His shoulders
flexed and went taut. He strained with the effort of
holding back, of letting her touch and taste and
breathe in his scent.

When they finally sank back onto the bed, she was
wet and ready, more than ready, for him. He anchored
his hands in her hair, tilted her head back, drew a
little whimper of protest.

"We may be in trouble here, Sabrina."

The rough growl barely penetrated her haze.
"What?"

"You know those deep waters we talked about?"

"What…? Oh. Yes."

"I guess I'd better admit that I'm in over my
head." His gruff admission cut a path straight to her
heart. "Way over my head."

She stared up at eyes awash with a tenderness that
stole what little was left of her breath. At that moment, Sabrina tumbled out of lust, slid right past long-
ing and landed smack in the middle of love. She felt
herself dropping. Was powerless to stop the free fall.
Didn't even try.

A piercing happiness welled in her chest, so sharp
and strong that she knew she'd never forget this moment, this instant in time. She wanted to tell him that
she felt the same way. She wanted to laugh in exul-

tation, sob with joy, but he entered her with a long, slow thrust that had her swallowing everything but a scream.

She was sure they'd take off then, that they'd shoot up to the moon like rockets, much as they'd soared to the afternoon sun. But he kept the pace of their loving so slow and so sweet and so magical that she was sobbing with the wonder of it long before it ended.

Despite her nap earlier, Sabrina never found out if Jack could make good on his boast to stay awake all night. Nor did they ever have their promised talk.

She felt herself slipping into oblivion after only an hour in his arms. Or maybe it was two. Or three. She couldn't find the strength to lift her head and check the clock.

She buried her face in the warm angle between his neck and shoulder. She didn't want to think about that damned clock. Didn't want to hold back the tides of sleep, the tides of love. But the sense of responsibility that followed her like a shadow kept her awake long enough to mutter into the warm skin under her lips.

"Jack..."

"I'm here."

"The alarm. Is it...is it set?"

He craned his neck. "Yes. Do you want me to turn it off?"

Her breath puffed out in a long sigh. "No. It's my

turn to open tomorrow. I'll have to get up at...four-thirty.''

''Four-thirty!''

''Mmm.''

A groan rumbled in his chest. ''Okay, Sleeping Beauty. You'd better go into your trance.''

''I...already...have.''

Chuckling, he drew her up a little higher on his shoulder.

That soft laugh and the smooth flex of his muscles under her cheek would constitute Sabrina's last real memories of Jack Wentworth.

Chapter 11

The soft, persistent hum jolted Jack right from sleep into instant wakefulness. He lay absolutely still, waiting while his senses made order of the noise and the darkness and the warm body curled into his.

It took him only a second or two to identify the hum, another couple to ease out of Sabrina's loose hold. Naked, he scooped up his jeans and dug a small, flat beeper out of the pocket. A single glance at the illuminated digits had his skin prickling.

He glanced at the phone on the nightstand beside the bed, then spun around and left the room. The door shut noiselessly behind him. Picking up the living room phone, he punched in a code to scramble the signal, then hammered out a ten-number sequence. Trey McGill answered on the second ring.

"El Jafir hit a refinery last night," the State Department rep said without preamble.

Jack swore, low and long. "Any casualties?"

"No, and no serious damage. But the bastards promised real fireworks next time."

"Dammit!"

"We need you on a plane today."

Before he thought about it, before he had time even to understand it, a protest formed in Jack's throat. He didn't want to leave Sabrina. Not now. Not until he'd satisfied his raw need to make her his.

Not even then.

Especially not then.

"I can't this time, Trey."

"What?"

The single syllable exploded with such astonished disbelief that Jack almost smiled.

"Send someone else."

"There isn't anyone else," Trey snarled. "No one that Prince Kaisal and his father trust after the damned leak."

"Have you found the source?"

"We've traced it back to State, but the trail ends there."

"Why doesn't that surprise me?"

Jack wasn't a fan of huge, amorphous organizations at the best of times…which was one of the reasons why he operated so well outside of them.

"Sounds like you've got some serious housecleaning to do," he bit out.

"We do. In the meantime, we've been hustling to put together the emergency aid package I told you about. We need you to take it in."

"Hell!"

Scowling at the dim outline of the Route 66 poster on the living room wall, Jack raked a hand through his hair. He had to do this. He had too many of his own people in Qatar, and he and Ali went too far back to let him down now. Deliberately, he shoved aside his gnawing reluctance.

"All right, I'm in."

"Good! You can use your concern over the security of the Wentworth Oil people in-country as a cover. I'll brief you on the aid package when you get to D.C. Do you want me to send an air force jet to pick you up?"

"No. I'll get my people to roll out the Lear. I'll be there in…"

He flicked a glance at his watch. He had to get to the office, retrieve his passport and some cash, establish a cover for the unexpected trip. As Trey had intimated, that wasn't a problem. The security of his people demanded his immediate, personal attention.

"I'll be there by ten your time," he said. "Noon at the latest."

"Good enough. In the meantime, I'll work the final details on the package."

"You'd damned well better work on getting some accurate intelligence on the situation in Qatar," Jack shot back. "I'm not going in blind, and I'm sure as hell not leaving my people in danger if the whole country's about to blow. And, Trey…?''

''Yeah?''

''This is the last time.''

A brief, charged silence spun out while McGill digested that.

''What's going on, Wentworth?''

Jack thought of the answers he could give. He'd met someone. Fallen for her, hard. Wanted her with a ferocity that had exploded into a shimmering, illusive emotion he'd never experienced before, never really believed in until Sabrina.

As it turned out, he didn't have to respond to Trey's question. McGill supplied his own answer.

''It's that Jensen woman, isn't it? She's gotten to you?''

''Yes.''

The silence this time was longer, and razor-edged with the memory of Heather. Finally, Trey blew out a low, shaky breath.

''I hope she knows what she's getting into.''

Jack's glance went to the hall and the dark bedroom beyond. ''She doesn't, but I'll make sure she does before we take it any further.''

''Yeah, well…good luck.''

''Thanks,'' Jack said quietly.

He cut the connection, then immediately dialed the twenty-four-hour Wentworth operations center. Tersely, he instructed the on-duty controller to put their people in Qatar on highest alert and to get the Learjet fueled and readied.

He dressed quickly. As always before these operations, his heart pumped pure adrenaline. This time, it also pumped a steady measure of regret. He bent a knee on the bed, smiling at the tight ball of woman in the center of the mattress.

"Sabrina."

She didn't stir. Didn't so much as blink. Gently, he shook her arm.

"Something's come up, sweetheart. I have to go."

"Mmm."

Still deep in slumber, she twitched and brought her knees up under her chin. Jack's mouth curved into a grin. He hadn't understated matters this afternoon. When this woman slept, she slept. Bending, he dropped a kiss on the tangled silk of her hair.

"I'll be back."

He carried her mumbled "mmm" out of the room and into the night.

Stars glittered like diamonds in the indigo sky as Jack drove the empty roads to Tulsa. He left the truck in the underground garage and took the elevator to the top floor of the Wentworth Building. The security guard on duty tensed when the doors hummed open, then immediately relaxed. He was too used to seeing Wentworth Oil's CEO at all hours to do more than nod and smile.

Less than fifteen minutes later, Jack had showered,

shaved and changed in the private bath just off his office. He was knotting his tie when an unshaven but otherwise impeccably dressed Peter Hastings strolled through the door to the executive suite, pen and steno pad in hand.

"You didn't have to come in." Jack voiced the protest, although he knew it was useless. "I planned to dictate instructions for you."

"The ops center called me," Pete said calmly. "What do you want me to do?"

Squaring the Windsor knot on his tie, Jack fired off the list he'd formulated during the quick drive to Tulsa.

"I didn't want to disturb my grandfather this early. Call him later this morning and explain about the attack on the refinery in Qatar. Tell him I'll contact him as soon as I'm comfortable with the security arrangement for our people."

"Done."

"Tell Hannah to expect me when she sees me."

"That will break her heart," Pete commented dryly.

Grinning, Jack tossed his briefcase onto his desk and snapped it open. He knew full well that his housekeeper would dance in delight at having the Tulsa apartment to herself for the foreseeable future.

"Make sure the ops center maintains real time communications link with our on-site supervisor in Qatar. I want to be advised immediately of any deterioration in the situation from their perspective."

Trey would provide State's assessment, as well, but Jack had learned long ago to pull in his own intelligence sources whenever possible.

He ran through the rest of his short list, then yanked open his desk drawer to retrieve his passport and the nickel-finished nine-shot Marakov he'd taken off a disgruntled Iraqi officer some years ago. Pete waited patiently while Jack checked the chamber, the clip and the spare magazine.

"Anything else?"

"No. I…"

Jack's gaze snagged on the photograph that had slipped to the back of the drawer. Sabrina's smiling face sent his heart into a quick, fast roll. He drew out the photo. Slowly, tenderly, he brushed a thumb across the glossy finish.

Lord, had it been less than a week since they'd posed for the picture at the Route 66 Blowout? It seemed longer. So much longer. Jack had to stretch to remember a time before Sabrina. A life before Sabrina.

He tucked the photo in one of the pockets in his briefcase.

"Yes," he told Pete. "There is something else. See if you can locate the owner of the jewelry store in the lobby. Ask him to meet me there in a half hour."

For one of the few times in their association, the unflappable former panhandler lost his flap. His jaw dropping, he gaped at his boss.

"Huh?"

"I don't have time to explain now, Pete. Just do it."

With vivid images of Sabrina as he'd left her tumbling through his mind, Jack scribbled a quick note on his personal stationery. He didn't know how long he'd be gone, and this time he wasn't taking any chances that she might think he skipped out on her.

Sabrina—
Our time together was magical. I need to see you, talk to you. I'll contact you as soon as I possibly can.

J.

With final instructions to Pete to track down Ms. Jensen and deliver the note if events in Qatar kept him out of the country for an extended period, he left the Wentworth Building forty-five minutes later. A sparkling, emerald-cut solitaire nestled in a blue velvet box in his briefcase, along with the Marakov and the picture of Sabrina. When he returned from Qatar, Jack thought with fierce satisfaction, he wouldn't have to waste time shopping for an engagement ring before making tracks directly to the diner.

He glanced at his watch, smiling when he saw the time. Sabrina's alarm clock was set to go off in a half hour. He was tempted to call her, just to hear her voice, but he didn't want to steal what little sleep she had left. He could see her in his mind, almost orchestrate every move in the scenario that would follow the shrill of the alarm.

She'd groan, slam a hand on the nightstand to turn the screech off, then stretch. He saw her uncurl those long, gorgeous legs. Heard her grumble into the pillow. Felt the kick in his gut as he thought about all the mornings he hoped to watch a lazy smile fill her green eyes as she came fully awake next to him.

At precisely four-thirty, a shrill buzz shocked Sabrina awake. Groaning, she stretched out an arm and thumped at the nightstand until she hit the alarm. Mercifully, the buzzing stopped.

She lay unmoving for a few moments, boneless and utterly content. Comfortable silence cocooned her. The rumpled sheets carried the faint scent of Jack's musky maleness. The pillow had bunched where he'd jammed it under his head. She closed her eyes, imagining him beside her, remembering the incredible night just past. If Sabrina had been asked to describe the way she felt at that precise moment, she would have said well and thoroughly loved.

Jack hadn't said the actual words. Nor had she, she remembered with a smile. They hadn't needed to. She'd seen the tenderness behind his smile and tasted hot desire in his kiss. The wellspring of passion she'd found in his arms stunned her whenever she thought about it.

Hazy fragments from the night drifted through her mind. She might have imagined that Jack had shaken her gently sometime during the night. She could have fantasized a kiss as soft as mist. But she couldn't have dreamed his whisper that something had come up, that he had to go.

That he'd come back.

Hugging the husky promise to herself, she rolled off the bed and went to shower. She drove to work on autopilot, her eyes on the road and her mind on Jack. A foolish, almost giddy happiness engulfed her. She felt as though she were the first woman to fall in love. The only one who'd ever glowed from the inside out with the knowledge that she was loved.

The glow stayed with her all through that muggy Thursday at the diner, and the night that followed. It was still warm when the phone at the diner shrilled on Friday morning. Peg snatched the receiver off the hook, then waved it in the air to catch Sabrina's attention.

"For you, kiddo."

Her heart jumped. Swiping her palms down the seam of her jeans, Sabrina grabbed the receiver and turned a shoulder on the noisy lunch crowd. She expected to hear Jack's voice. She hoped that he'd tell her he was on the way back from wherever he'd taken off to, that he wanted her, that he loved her.

Instead, a cool, briskly efficient bank official identified himself. "It's my pleasure to inform you that your small business loan has been approved, Ms. Jensen."

"Are you serious?"

"Completely."

Sabrina's joyous whoop bounced off the diner's wall. The caller waited until she'd calmed down to continue.

"You'll have to come in and review the terms and conditions of the loan, of course, but I'm sure you'll find them most satisfactory. Would this afternoon be convenient for you?"

"This afternoon?" Grinning, she twirled the phone cord around her hand. "When you folks make up your mind, you don't waste time, do you?"

"Not if we can help it. Of course, we like to expedite matters when the applicant has your connections," he added unctuously.

She blinked. "What connections? What are you talking about?"

"Let's just say the instructions to approve your loan came directly from Wentworth corporate headquarters, and since the corporation owns our bank…" His voice trailed off delicately.

"I see."

"So, what time this afternoon would be convenient for you?"

"I'll have to get back to you."

"Fine. I'm at your disposal. May I give you my name and phone number?"

"What? Oh, yes, of course."

Pulling a stubby pencil from her pocket, Sabrina jotted down the information before clicking the receiver back onto its rack. The elation that had filled her only moments ago now felt a little flat.

Why in the world did it matter that Jack had intervened? The loan was a matter of business, after all. If she was going to succeed in the world of commerce and high finance, she shouldn't balk at using her connections.

She just hadn't thought of Jack Wentworth as a connection.

Unable to shrug aside the awkward feeling, she decided to wait to tell Hank about the loan approval until she had a chance to talk to Jack. She'd let him know that she appreciated his help, but...well, she didn't want to plunge into a relationship by taking advantage of his name. That was the plan, anyway...until Hank pushed through the swinging door late that afternoon.

Sabrina took one look at his face and gasped. Sliding the tray she was carrying onto the counter, she rushed to his side.

"Are you all right?"

"I'm okay, but..."

"But what, Hank?"

"I just heard...on the radio..."

"What?"

He moved his well-chewed cigar from one side of his mouth to the other, then tossed it into the trash can. His face creased with compassion. Groping for her hand, he held on tight.

"It's that Wentworth fellow, the one who polished the floor with my pork chops the other night."

"Jack?" she said foolishly, as if she knew any other Wentworth. "What about Jack?"

"He's dead, Sabrina. He died in a terrorist attack, they said, over in one of those Arab oil countries."

Chapter 12

Long agonizing weeks later, when Sabrina could think of Jack without sobs tearing at the back of her throat, she would realize that a part of her died, too, in the shocked stillness of that June afternoon. The pain that pierced her when she heard about the terrorist attack and explosion on an offshore rig off the coast of Qatar was so sharp, so searing, that she was sure she couldn't hurt anymore. She soon discovered how wrong she was.

Her friends tried to comfort her. Hank and Peg and the regulars who'd met Jack at the diner shook their heads. What a shame, they murmured. He seemed like an all right kind of guy, despite his less than stellar performance as a waiter. None of them, of course, had any idea how fast and hard Sabrina had fallen for Jack Wentworth, or how much a part of her he'd become.

Even her twin didn't suspect. Rachel knew next to nothing about Jack, had no idea how swiftly he'd claimed her sister's closely guarded heart. She only knew that her twin was hurting.

Then suddenly, just when Sabrina was starting to accept that she'd always live with an aching sense of loss for what might have been, the rest of her world began to crash in on her, piece by piece.

The first inkling of what was to come occurred less than a week after Jack's death. Sapped of energy by the heat and the constant ache she carried just under her heart, Sabrina drove home from work and pulled into the driveway. The car's engine rattled and coughed before choking into stillness. She sat for a moment, trying to summon the will to open the car door.

Finally, the heat rising in shimmering waves all around her drove her out of the car and into the house. The quiet dimness inside should have been a relief. Instead, it echoed emptily. She'd no sooner dumped her purse on the kitchen table than she caught sight of the dented Harlow poster and box of light fixtures from the old motor court. She hadn't had time to do anything with them before Jack's death. Afterward...

Her eyes closed. Tears burned the back of her lids.

"Dammit!"

Planting both hands on the counter, Sabrina fought the hot splash of tears. She had to get a grip. She couldn't continue to hurt every time she remembered their short time together. Every time she thought about Jack's smile, or heard the echo of his laugh, or remembered how her heart had splintered into a million shards the night he'd massaged her aching feet.

She was still fighting the hot sting of tears when the doorbell rang. Shuddering, she drew in a long, shaky breath and went to answer it. She didn't recognize the sandy-haired man on the porch. Cautious and in no mood for visitors, she kept the latched screen door between them.

"Ms. Jensen?"

"Yes?"

"My name is Trey McGill."

"Yes?"

"I'm a friend..." His gray eyes darkened for a moment, then he corrected himself gently. "I was a friend of Jack's."

Sabrina's throat closed. She clutched the door, unable to speak.

"I was with Jack in Washington right before he flew out to Qatar, Ms. Jensen. I thought you might want to know that he was thinking of you."

That didn't make it easier, Sabrina discovered as a series of small tremors shook her. Her hand trembling, she unlatched the screen door.

"Did you come all the way from Washington just to tell me that, Mr. McGill?"

"Trey, please."

He followed her inside and breathed a long sigh of relief as she shut the heat out. Declining her offer of iced tea, he took a swift look around the living room before turning to face her.

"In answer to your question, no, I didn't come just to tell you that. I'm with the State Department."

He paused, as if that should impress her or mean something special. When Sabrina simply stared at him, he speared a hand through his short, sandy hair and elaborated on his mission.

"I flew out to Oklahoma to meet with the Wentworths."

"They must be devastated," she murmured.

"They are." Compassion threaded through her visitor's voice, faintly tipped with its East Coast accent. "And Joseph Wentworth is mad as hell. He seems to think the United States should be moving faster on the identification of his grandson's remains."

Sabrina flinched at the stark, disembodied term. Was that all that was left of someone so vital, so full of life as Jack?

She'd watched the early TV reports, hoping, praying they were wrong. A single glimpse of the satellite image of the fiery inferno engulfing the offshore rig had shredded those hopes completely. The blast had been so fearsome, so all-consuming, that it had taken firefighters long, agonizing days to cap the blaze spewing pillars of black smoke into the sky. According to the most recent news reports, identification of the victims had just begun.

Trey caught her stricken expression and cursed softly under his breath. "I'm sorry. This is hard for you. I didn't mean to make it worse. I just wanted to assure you that Jack cared for you, far more than the others.''

Others? She controlled another flinch. Of course, there had been others. Jack Wentworth didn't walk the walk or talk the talk of a monk. Sabrina just didn't particularly want to hear about any women he might have loved right now. Before she could tell Trey so, though, he rushed to reassure her.

''Jack and I went back a long way. I've seen him connect with a lot of women. None of them got close to him, though. Not the way you did, Ms. Jensen.''

''Sabrina,'' she murmured. ''Call me Sabrina. He talked about me? About us?''

''Not directly. Jack wasn't the kind to talk about his personal life.'' McGill's mouth twisted. ''He wouldn't even talk about Heather to me.''

The question slipped out before Sabrina could stop it. ''Who's Heather?''

Surprise blanked his face. ''He didn't tell you?''

''No.''

He hesitated, obviously wishing he'd kept his mouth shut. Just when Sabrina decided he wasn't going to answer, he forced out a short, stiff explanation.

''Heather Blake was a Washington attorney. She loved Jack, and she died because of it.''

The denial came fast and instinctively. ''I don't believe it.''

''Oh, they ruled her death an accident,'' he said swiftly, almost bitterly. ''A fatal mix of drugs and alcohol. I know Jack didn't mean to hurt her, or leave her alone and wondering what she'd done wrong. He cared about her…just as he cared about you. I had to come, to make sure you knew that."

Stunned, Sabrina could only stare at him.

"That bank loan Jack arranged for you wasn't a pricey brush-off," Trey insisted fiercely. "He didn't mean it that way, whatever his people might have told you."

"They didn't… I didn't…"

She stumbled for words, her mind whirling. Jack had told McGill about the loan? Why hadn't he told *her?* Why had he left it to some smarmy bank official, who couldn't resist smirking about her special "relationship" with the Wentworths?

Caught up in a swirl of confusion, Sabrina watched as her visitor slipped an embossed card out of his pocket. When he reached out and pressed her fingers around it, she stared at it blankly.

"I know all this is hard for you to deal with now. Call me if you need someone to talk to, or if old man Wentworth starts giving you grief."

"Jack's grandfather?" Her numb fingers curled around the slip of shiny cardboard. "Why should Mr. Wentworth give me grief?"

Trey paused with his hand on the doorknob, weighing his words.

"Look, I don't want to scare you," he said slowly, "but I think you should know Joseph Wentworth is as ruthless as they come. He peddled a lot of influence and a whole lot of oil dollars to keep the Wentworth name out of the papers after Heather's death. He wouldn't appreciate seeing you sell your story or any intimate pictures of you and Jack to the tabloids before his grandson's body is even brought home for burial.''

She reeled, stunned anew by the very thought. "I wouldn't go to the press! I wouldn't try to make money off Jack's death!''

"No, I didn't think you would.'' His gray eyes gentled, filled once more with compassion. "Just watch yourself, Sabrina, and call me if you ever need help. As I said, Jack and I went back a long way.''

The insidious doubts began to eat at Sabrina that very night.

Trey had sworn that Jack had cared for her. She would have sworn that he'd loved her, however briefly. But had she read too much into his passionate kisses? Heard more than he'd intended in his smiling declaration the last night they were together?

Oh, God, was that damned bank loan his way of saying it was fun, and thanks for the memories? The possibility tied her stomach in knots.

Old doubts came rushing back with the new. Could Jack Wentworth really have fallen for someone so different from the sleek, cultured women who frequented his own circle? Even the tragic attorney Trey had told her about hadn't been able to hold the elusive oil executive's interest. Looking back at their time together, Sabrina realized that Jack had met most of her friends, but introduced her to few of his. He'd never even invited her home to meet his grandfather or the brother and sister he'd told her about.

Maybe he'd been ashamed of her. Maybe he'd just been whiling away some long summer days...and nights...with the so-accommodating waitress. Maybe he hadn't loved her, as she'd loved him.

Like a complete idiot, Sabrina didn't understand the reason for the unremitting hunger pangs that attacked her night and day until almost the middle of July. Finally, the truth hit her.

She was pregnant.

The realization came early one morning, while she was getting ready for work. She stepped into her favorite jeans and got them over her hips, but she was darned if she could get them snapped. She struggled with them for several moments before giving up in disgust.

Grumbling, she kicked off the too-tight pair and rooted through her closet for something looser. From all she'd read, grief destroyed most people's appetite. In contrast, she'd been wolfing down double helpings at the diner, except for those days she'd felt too queasy to—

Suddenly, she froze. Her mind went absolutely blank, then strung together the symptoms she'd paid no attention to until this moment. Lethargy. Constant hunger. Unexpected bouts of queasiness.

No! No, she couldn't be...!

She thought back to her last period. Her breath left on a whoosh.

Oh, God, she was!

The certainty grabbed her by the throat. Sabrina shook from head to toe with shock, disbelief and a wild, singing joy. She carried Jack's child. She sank onto the bed and burst into tears.

She was still sobbing when she snatched up the phone to call her twin.

"You're what!"

Rachel's yelp raised a misty smile.

"Pregnant. I'm pregnant, Rach. At least, I think so."

A charged silence followed while Rachel assimilated the news. Sabrina tried not to sniffle into the phone. Finally, her sister probed cautiously.

"Is the father anyone I know?"

Pain kicked at Sabrina's heart. "No. He's...he's gone, Rachel."

"You mean he's left you alone to deal with this? Nice guy," she said in disgust. "So how do you feel about the baby?"

"Other than weepy and in shock?"

"Other than that."

She flopped back onto the bed. Fresh tears streamed down her cheeks. She recognized them for what they were.

"Joyous. I feel joyous."

"Then I do, too," Rachel declared before she, too, burst into tears.

The two sisters laughed and cried and laughed some more until they ran out of breath for both. Happy and scared and more than a little overwhelmed, Sabrina stared at the ceiling.

"What about your plans to buy the diner?" Rachel asked. "And the classes you were going to take this fall?"

"What about them?"

"Are you going to press ahead?"

"Definitely. I want my degree and I want to buy the diner. More than ever now." And Sabrina knew she had the means to do it. She hadn't returned the unctuous bank officer's calls. Nor had she gone to Tulsa to review the terms and conditions of the loan. Jack's death, and the slicing little doubt about why he'd greased the skids had made her put her dreams on hold.

She couldn't let those doubts stand in her way now. For whatever reasons of his own, Jack had made it possible for her to buy the diner. She'd use the loan he arranged as collateral for her child's future.

Their child's future.

"Are you going to tell the father's family about the baby?"

Rachel's quiet question triggered a whole new set of concerns. Unbidden, Trey McGill's warning echoed in Sabrina's mind.

"Not yet," she said slowly.

"They'd want to know. They have a right to know, Sabrina."

She bit her lip. She didn't want to share her baby with anyone except her twin just yet. Especially not with a man Trey McGill had labeled as completely ruthless. Even if she did, Joseph Wentworth might not believe the baby was his great-grandchild. He might think she was trying to play on his grief, or attempting to cash in on Jack's estate. No, she wasn't ready to face that yet.

"It's too soon to tell them. I'm not even sure myself. I'm just making an uninformed assumption at this point."

"Well find out, for heaven's sake. Go get one of those little home pregnancy tests, and call me right back! Better yet, maybe I'll drive over tomorrow and we'll take the test together."

Sabrina shot upright. "Rachel, you're not...?"

"No way! I haven't met a man yet I'd want to make babies with."

"I didn't exactly plan on making this baby," Sabrina said softly, fiercely. "But I'm glad, *so* glad we did."

After that, events seemed to rush forward with the horrifying velocity of a high-powered, high-speed, out-of-control train.

Sabrina started seeing as well as feeling the subtle changes in her body. An OB/GYN from out-of-the-way Mason's Grove prescribed megadoses of prenatal vitamins. Confused and still not ready to approach the Wentworths, she called Trey McGill to ask his advice.

After a brief, tense silence, McGill painted an even more detailed picture of Joseph Wentworth's forceful personality and ruthless determination to control his vast empire and everyone in it. Sabrina lay awake for several nights, debating whether to contact Jack's grandfather.

Then she heard a news report that the Wentworth family was attempting to identify a woman in a photograph they'd found among his personal effects.

The photo flashed on the TV screen. It was her, Sabrina saw with a ripple of shock. Shaken, she knew she had to come forward, to let the Wentworths know she carried Jack's baby.

She fully intended to call them the next morning…until a car with darkened windows tried to force the Mazda off the road into a water-filled ditch. That same evening, a masked figure broke into her home. Sabrina fled out the back door and spent the next several months alone and terrified and running for her life.

She didn't stop running until utter desperation forced her to accept the aid of the man she feared would take her baby. Even then, she couldn't shake her fear.

Not when Joseph Wentworth offered her the sanctuary of the stone gatekeeper's cottage.

Not when her daughter was born three weeks ago,

healthy and hale, with blue eyes so like Jack's that Sabrina's heart broke all over again.

Not now, especially not now, with the cold March rain weeping against the windows and a gaunt, bearded ghost staring at her from the shadows on the other side of her baby's bassinet.

Chapter 13

"I came back, Sabrina." A muscle worked in the side of Jack's face. "I promised you I would. The night I left."

Oh, God! How could she ache for him? How could she want his touch so desperately, and at the same time feel her fingers curling into claws at the thought of his hands on her body? How could he raise a flood of heat in her belly with that twisted smile, even as she furtively searched the room for her purse with its concealed handgun?

Then he lifted a hand and took a half step toward her. The memories, the pain, even the agonizing shock of his return vaporized. All that was left was the fear that had driven her for so long, for so many tortured miles. She gathered her muscles, preparing to dive sideways, to snatch up her purse, to fumble inside it for the concealed 9 mm Beretta.

Jack's low, harsh voice held her where she stood. "I won't hurt you, Sabrina. You or the baby. You don't need a gun to protect yourself from me."

Her entire body quivered. "How do you know I have a gun?"

"My grandfather told me."

Her breath hissed out. "You've talked to your grandfather?"

"I didn't know you were here. I went straight to the big house."

"And he sent you here?"

For the first time since he'd stepped out of the shadows, Jack's face lost some of its stark, unrelenting cast.

"When he recovered from the shock of seeing a dead man walk into his bedroom, he told me to haul my butt over to the guest house…and to make sure I didn't get shot in the process. He let me know in no uncertain terms that he wasn't about to conduct two memorial services for the same grandson in less than a year."

Sabrina lifted a trembling hand to push her hair from her forehead. Joseph had sent him to her. Even after all that had happened in the past months. Even knowing she'd do anything to protect her child from the nameless, faceless killer who'd almost taken her life and the baby's.

"What else did he tell you?"

Jack's glance went to the bassinet, then came back to Sabrina.

"Nothing."

Her head whirled. Joseph had left it to her to tell Jack what she would, just as he'd kept her hidden and safe these past few weeks while the family friend Josie Wentworth had implored to find Sabrina and the sheriff Rachel had tumbled into love with had joined forces to discover who wanted her and her child dead.

Sam Arquette and Riley Hunter were still tracking the culprit. Sabrina's heart twisted with sharp, lancing pain. Could he be standing right here before her?

Joseph obviously didn't think so, or he wouldn't have sent his grandson to the guest cottage. Sabrina didn't want to think so, either. She longed to throw herself into Jack's arms, to sob out her joy at his return and share the miracle of their daughter. She fought the need with everything that was in her.

Until she knew where he'd gone and why the heck he'd let her believe him dead all these months, she couldn't, wouldn't, trust him. Only one thing motivated Sabrina as she dove for her purse. The baby came first. She had to.

In a swift, practiced move, she pulled the Beretta from its holster. Her hand didn't waver as she held the weapon steady on Jack. She'd spent enough hours at the firing range after she'd purchased the gun to know how to use it.

"Move away from the baby, Jack. Move away, and

we'll talk. You'll have to tell me where you've been all these months before I'll trust you near my child.''

She might have imagined the brief softening in his face a few seconds ago. At her low, urgent command, it became a mask again, so stark and tight that his cheekbones jutted below ice blue eyes as cold as death.

The fire crackled and snapped in the massive stone hearth. The rain beat against the windows. Jack's chest rose and fell under his hooded navy sweatshirt, once, twice. Then slowly, so slowly, he moved to the side, away from the bassinet.

''Where have you been?'' she demanded in a low, rasping voice. ''Why did you let us think you were dead all these months?''

''I was dead,'' he said flatly. ''Dead and buried. For most of the time, anyway.''

She steeled herself against the emptiness in his eyes and voice. ''Go on.''

He stared at her, his body coiled and tense under the sweatshirt. The words came slowly, as though dragged from a well he didn't want to tap.

''I don't remember much of the first few months. The explosion blinded me for a while, and they kept the bandages on as a blindfold for a long time after that.''

She swallowed. ''They?''

''*El Jafir.*'' His lip made a thin curl. ''That's what they style themselves. The Wind. They want to blow all the evil Western influence from their land. They call themselves true believers, but they're simply a loose confederation of sadistic fanatics with no agenda but terror. They blew the rig and everyone on it.''

"But…" She dragged in a jagged breath. "But we were told there were no survivors, that the explosion killed everyone on the rig."

"The blast blew at least two of us into the water. Maybe more." Firelight flickered on his unshaven face. A muscle ticked in one cheek. "But I'm the only one who crawled out of the pit."

Icy chills rippled down Sabrina's spine. This wasn't Jack. Not her Jack. He wasn't the same man she'd found smiling down at her when she opened her eyes that long-ago June afternoon. Or the same man who'd waded into a brawl with two drunken truckers. Or even the one who'd launched himself through the air to protect her from a falling roof. In the past, agonizing months, she'd remembered every moment of their days together, recounted his every expression, from laughter to pensive thought to the desperate fear of that moment in the motor court. Never, ever could she have envisioned the look she saw in his eyes now.

"What pit, Jack?"

He didn't answer for long moments. Then the words dragged out of him, slowly, hollowly.

"After the first few months, they kept us in a hole. They weren't interested in ransom, didn't even care about letting the rest of the world know we were alive. They simply wanted us to suffer, to live in darkness and reflect on the evil our insatiable greed for oil had wrought. They wanted us to know that we already inhabited our grave.''

''How…how did you get out?''

He stared at her for long, silent moments. Images only he could see drew the skin taut on his cheekbones. Then he shook his head with slow, absolute finality.

''I got out. That's all that matters.''

She had just started to breathe again when his next words sent shock ripping through her lungs.

''That,'' he said softly, ''and the fact that the terrorists timed the explosion to the exact moment I stepped on that rig.''

''What?''

''I only stopped on the mainland long enough to see Ali and leave my briefcase and travel gear with him. A helicopter was already preflighted and waiting to take me out to the rig. It blew just as the helo touched down. From what my captors let drop, someone tipped them off that I was on that bird.''

''Ali?'' she breathed.

''I wondered,'' he growled. ''For a long time, I wondered. I had plenty of time to think in that hole. I paid a very private visit to the prince before I left Qatar.''

Sabrina struggled to understand how the dark-eyed, mustachioed prince who'd good-naturedly vied with

Jack for her attention last summer could have arranged the death of his friend.

"It wasn't him," Jack said, putting that specter to
rest. "But whoever tipped off the terrorists was the
same individual who paid those supposedly drunken
truckers to run down Ali and me."

"That was deliberate?" Sabrina's jaw sagged.

"That's the way I figured it."

"But who…? Why…?" His intent, piercing stare
raised a violent protest. "Oh, God, Jack, you can't
think *I* had anything to do with that attack? That I
wanted you dead?"

The hand holding the Beretta shook. Maybe that
explained the subsequent attempt to force her car off
the road. And the masked intruder who'd broken into
her house the night she'd fled. Maybe someone had
thought she'd contributed to Jack's death, had been
paid to set him up. Maybe they'd wanted to even the
score.

"No!"

The savage exclamation sliced through her chaotic
thoughts.

"I never thought it was you, Sabrina," Jack said
fiercely. "You kept me sane all those months. Your
face, your smile, the memory of how you looked that
day in Sapulpa, the way you curl into a tight ball
when you sleep."

He moved toward her.

Shell-shocked, her mind whirling, she brought the
gun up and leveled it at his chest. She'd been through

too much, had lived too long in fear to trust even her own instincts at this moment.

"Stop!"

"You were with me in that black hole, Sabrina. You were with me after I escaped and the desert almost finished what those bastards started."

Deliberately, he rounded the end of the sofa. She retreated, almost stumbling over her textbook and the black-and-orange OSU throw she'd tossed aside.

"Jack, wait!"

"I wanted to marry you. I even bought a ring the morning I left for Qatar."

"Josie showed me the ring. It was in the box she got of your personal effects, but I...I wasn't sure. I couldn't know...."

"All those months, I dreamed of you. Only you."

"I have to think! I have to..."

"I've done enough thinking to last a lifetime, Sabrina. Now..."

To her utter astonishment, his mouth curved! She shivered with confusion and fear and the horror of what he'd told her...and Jack grinned! Sabrina couldn't believe it, couldn't comprehend how he could transform so swiftly from a haunted, shadowy ghost to the man she'd dreamed about and cried over and ached to hold just once more all these agonizing months since his death.

"Now," he said softly, "I have to take you in my arms. I have to kiss you. The only way you can stop me is to shoot me."

"I will!" she warned fiercely. "Take another step and I will!"

The utter implacability in her voice brought him up short. Either that, or the snicker of metal on metal as she cocked the Beretta.

"You weren't the only one who went through hell! I did too, Jack. After you disappeared, someone tried to drive me off the road."

"What!"

"Someone tried to kill me," she whispered, her throat raw. "Me and the baby."

Every muscle in his body whipped wire-tight. His gaze cut from her to the bassinet. When his head swung toward her again, she could almost feel the heat from the blaze in the blue eyes that had been so cold and flat only a few moments ago.

"If you think I'd harm you or our child, you might as well pull that trigger now."

"How do you know that she's yours?" Desperation gave her voice a shrill edge. "We only had those few days together."

"You want me to ask?" he bit out, a red flush staining the cheeks above his beard. "You want me to demand a DNA test?"

"No!"

"Good, because I don't intend to. Dammit, I don't need to."

He closed the distance between them in two long strides. In those two strides, Sabrina had to choose between her head and her heart, between instinct and uncertainty, between the man who'd claim his child without a single instant of hesitation and the doubts that had driven her to despair these past months.

She barely had time to raise the pistol and flick on the safety before his hand closed over hers. The weapon slid from her grasp. Jack dropped it on the table at the end of the sofa, then speared his fingers through her tumbled hair. Sabrina didn't move, didn't protest as he pulled her head back.

"I'm going to kiss you," he warned savagely. "Hard and long. Then I'm going to hold my daughter. Then we'll talk. You'll tell me what the hell's been going on in the past nine months, and I'll try to figure out what the hell we're going to do about it."

Rough beard scraped her chin. Rough hands tugged at her scalp. He kissed her, hard...and long.

After the first heart-stopping seconds, Sabrina rose up on her toes, strained against him, locked her arms around his neck. Her own urgent need pushed the contact from a one-sided, bruising kiss to a cleansing. A healing. A mingling of her tears and his low, raw groans. A sharing of pain, of laughter, of the burning need that had brought them together so many months ago.

If Sabrina had still harbored any doubts after she raised her head, panting and wholly, joyously alive for the first time since that awful day she'd been told Jack was dead, they would have shredded the instant he slid his hands under the small, sleepy bundle who was their daughter and lifted her to the light.

"What's her name?" he asked softly.

"Elizabeth. I call her Beth."

He shot her a startled look. "That was my mother's name."

"I know. Joseph told me."

It was also his new sister-in-law's name, but the sight of Jack gazing raptly at his daughter made Sabrina's throat ache so much she couldn't share that bit of information with him. All she could do was tuck away in her heart the emotions that chased across his face, one after another.

There was awe. Amazement. A touch of wariness.

When a small, crinkled fist came up to rub against a scrunched-up nose, Jack shook his head in wonder. Eyes suspiciously bright, he studied each tiny, perfect finger with its tiny, perfect knuckle and tiny, perfect nail. Then Beth jerked into a little ball, stretched out again, and lifted her tiny, perfect lids.

"Her eyes are blue," he announced, as though the baby's mother wasn't perfectly well aware of that fact. "She's got my eyes."

Sabrina didn't have the heart to tell him that a newborn's eye color could and often did change. She watched, mesmerized, as he hefted the little bundle of blankets and baby up higher. By the light of the glowing fire, father and daughter studied each other.

"My eyes, but your chin and hair and incredible skin," Jack murmured. "She's a beauty. Something tells me she's going to wrap my grandfather around her little finger.''

"She already has," Sabrina confirmed with a teary smile. "Along with my father, my sister, your sister, your brother, and your assorted in-laws."

He turned toward her, his face blank.

"In-laws?"

She saw that she'd thrown him for a complete loop. "Didn't your grandfather fill you in on anything of what happened while you were…while you were…?"

"Dead?" he supplied dryly. "No. All he told me was to haul my butt over to the guest house and not get shot in the process."

How like Joseph to leave her to explain how Jack's sister, Josie, had come in search of Sabrina at her cousin's ranch, then ended up falling in love with the once grouchy, bad-tempered Max; how Jack's old friend, Sam Arquette, had tracked Sabrina down to Dr. Amanda Lucas's office; how Rachel had posed as Sabrina and led Sheriff Riley Hunter on a merry chase; how even Jack's playboy younger brother, Michael, had become caught up in the chase and proposed a marriage of convenience to the very young, very pregnant woman he subsequently tumbled head over heels in love with.

She started to tell Jack about his host of new relatives, and that he would meet them soon. The clan was gathering at the main house for dinner less than an hour from now. They were coming to attend Beth's christening ceremony this weekend.

But all that could wait. Right now, Jack needed a few moments with his daughter and Sabrina needed to watch them together. Just watch them. Then, she decided with a misty smile, they'd have the talk they were always promising to have and never seemed to get around to.

As it turned out, the explanations took a back seat to other, more immediate requirements. Beth had to be fed and changed. Jack scraped his hand across his chin and declared that his priorities at that moment included a cup of steaming hot coffee, a quick shower and another dozen or so kisses, not necessarily in that order.

Her heart and her mind still whirling, Sabrina tucked a gurgling, bright-eyed Beth back in her bassinet and provided the kisses. Finally, she ordered Jack to the upstairs bathroom and started for the kitchen. Instincts too strong for her to overcome wouldn't let her leave the baby alone, even for the few moments it would take to fill the coffeemaker.

Someone had tried to kill Jack.

Someone had tried to kill her.

That someone had yet to be identified.

For a long time, Sabrina had worried that perhaps one of the Wentworths wanted to destroy her, afraid that her child would cut them out of an inheritance. Or someone from Jack's past had come after her, angered over a business deal gone sour or lucrative oil leases snatched up under his or her nose. Right up until the moment she'd given birth, Sabrina had feared that Joseph Wentworth would use his considerable wealth and influence to take the baby from her.

Those fears hadn't been groundless or the neurotic imaginings of a desperate woman. She could still remember Trey McGill's tense silence when she'd called him to ask his advice soon after she learned she was pregnant. Too late, she'd understood the reason behind his reticence.

Gradually she'd learned that Jack had led a double life not even his family knew about, that he'd carried out secret missions for the government for years. The astounding bits and pieces of his other life had come out during the long, terrible months after his death, when Joseph and Josie and Michael had turned heaven and earth to find her. They'd been as astonished as Sabrina to learn the real reason for Prince Fashor's visit to Oklahoma last summer, just as they'd discovered that more than concern for the security of Wentworth employees had taken Jack to Qatar.

The knowledge of his double life had handed Sabrina a whole new set of fears. The terrorists who'd killed him might have had a personal vendetta against him...which they'd extended to his child.

That was the reason she'd ultimately accepted Joseph Wentworth's offer of sanctuary. The government hadn't been able to protect Jack, one of its own operatives. After Beth's birth, Joseph promised Sabrina and her child the safety of state-of-the-art security systems and round-the-clock ground patrols.

Still, she rolled the bassinet into the kitchen with her when she went to make a pot of coffee.

Chapter 14

Jack stood under the shower head, palms flattened against the tiles, head bowed. Hot, almost scalding water needled his back and shoulders. The pelting bullets cleansed his body, but he knew it would take more than water to sluice away the memory of the fear he'd seen in Sabrina's eyes when she'd leveled that gun at him.

Her terse account of what she'd been through in the past year played and replayed in his mind. Jaws tight, he tried to pull his rioting thoughts together. He needed to shut out every emotion. He had to get past their tumultuous reunion. Think beyond the shock, the wonder, of knowing he had a child. He needed to focus his energies, concentrate his thoughts, as he'd taught himself to do during those months in hell.

He'd had nothing else to do but focus then. Closing his eyes against the streaming water, Jack thought of all the hours, days, weeks he'd spent recalling old nursery rhymes, retracing treks through winter-browned fields to quail hunt with his grandfather, remembering the childish squabbles he'd arbitrated between his sister and brother.

He'd relived his childhood, year by year, then his adulthood. He'd thought through the mistakes he'd made, wished he'd taken a different approach to problems a time or two, but whenever bitterness or fury or despair threatened to choke him, Jack reminded himself that all the paths he'd taken in his life had led ultimately to Sabrina. That realization alone could lighten the blackness. His implacable determination to get home to her, and to his family, had kept him alive.

Now he'd returned…only to find Sabrina battling the same demons who'd haunted him. Fear. Suspicion. Threats to her life. A desperation that put shadows under her eyes and a gun in her hand.

Jack cursed, low and long and viciously. He had a good idea who'd loosed those demons.

It had taken him a while, but he'd finally put a name and a face to his betrayer. He'd started by cataloguing everyone who might have wanted to arrange his death. One by one, he'd sorted through the enemies he'd made during his covert work. The executives he'd cut out of a deal. His friends. Even Ali, who could have wanted to demonstrate to the revolutionaries that he'd seen the error of his ways and wanted to rid Qatar of Western influence once and for all. During his darkest hours, though, Jack hadn't been able to bring himself to add his family to the list. Or Sabrina.

Gradually, painfully, he'd narrowed the names, until there was only one left.

Trey McGill.

Trey had pressured Jack into taking this last mission. Trey had coordinated the flight from D.C. into Qatar. Trey, through his contacts at the consulate, had arranged the helo to take Jack out to the oil rig.

Once he'd focused on those pieces of the puzzle, others fell into place. Trey had also known about the stop at the Route 66 diner that hot, sunny afternoon in June. Jack himself had called and notified McGill of their stopover. The attack by the drunken truckers had come only a few hours later. At the time, Jack had assumed Ali was the intended target.

Now, he knew better.

Trey had wanted him dead.

Had he also tried to kill Sabrina and the baby?

Jack would know the answer to that question within the next twenty-four hours. First, though, he had to get his woman and his child out of the line of fire.

Willing himself to iron calm, he twisted off the taps. He left the hooded navy sweatshirt on the bed, opting for only the wrinkled white shirt he'd worn under it and the black slacks Ali had provided. A few moments later, he walked into the kitchen.

Sabrina glanced up from the sandwich she was making and bit her lip. The gaunt, bearded ghost who'd stepped out of the shadows had disappeared. In his place was a man she hardly recognized.

His tobacco brown hair laid dark and damp against his head. He was wearing the same wrinkled slacks and white cotton shirt he'd had on before, but he'd used her razor to scrape away the rough, scraggly beard. Without it, he should have looked cleaner, healthier, more familiar. Instead, the hollows under his cheekbones and the coiled tension in his shoulders only emphasized the hard-edged stranger he'd become.

For an odd moment, he seemed out of place in the warm, cheerful kitchen. She had the sense of a hunter poised to go in search of its prey. Or a wanderer who found himself in uncharted territory.

And no wonder! After months in darkness, the kitchen must seem like a different world to him. Like everything else in the eight-room guest house, it had been elegantly furnished at the time of construction and modernized several times over the years. Copper pots and a scattering of hand-painted crockery added a counterpoint of color to the dark ceiling beams and pine cabinetry imported, Sabrina had learned, from a seaside Tuscan villa. High-backed stools cushioned in bright yellow-and-red plaid invited lounging at the massive cook island, inset with gleaming Italian tiles. The same print curtained the casement windows and held the early March chill at bay. It was a comfortable, charming room, but Sabrina felt anything but comfortable as she stared at the whipcord lean stranger who met her gaze across the room.

Her heart twisted with the painful truth she'd been struggling to assimilate. This wasn't the man she'd loved so briefly, so intensely last summer. Could she love the person he now was? Would he love the woman she'd become?

Her hands shaky, she nudged a plate across the tiled island that ran the length of the kitchen. "I...I made you a sandwich. I thought you might be hungry."

"I am."

He came around the counter, his eyes feasting on her. He wanted more than food, she saw, her pulse leaping in response. His arms went around her. His mouth came down on hers. She went up on tiptoe, meeting his raw hunger, feeding on it.

Another moment, another kiss, and the past might have been vanquished once and for all. But a gurgling little hiccup broke through her sensual haze. Sabrina pulled back, shaking, and went to check the baby. Jack stood beside her at the bassinet. The same wonder that had crossed his face when he'd held Beth earlier settled over his features once again as he stared down at the infant.

"God, she's beautiful."

The new mother wouldn't argue with that. "Yes, she is. Even more beautiful than the day she was born."

He brushed a knuckle down a cloud-soft cheek. "Was it a tough birth?"

She dismissed thirty-two hours of grinding, panting labor with a little shrug. "Not as tough as what you went through."

His eyes raised to hers. Anger and frustration over what they'd missed flushed his cheeks. "I wish I'd been with you."

"Me, too."

"Next time."

The fierce promise set her heart somersaulting. The Sabrina of ten months ago would have melted in his arms again. The woman she was now took a deep breath and said what needed saying.

"Maybe it's too soon to talk about next time, Jack. Maybe we should take things slow and not...not commit to anything until we've had time to get to know each other again."

He shook his head. "We tried slow, remember? It didn't work."

"We've got a child to consider this time. We have to be sure, for her sake."

"I am sure, Sabrina."

Sliding a warm, hard palm into her hair, he tilted her face. She saw the absolute certainty in his eyes.

"I wanted to marry you last June, and I want to marry you now."

Her fingers curled into the wrinkled shirt. "You've been through so much. We both have. We're not the same people we were in June. Even then, we barely knew each other!''

"I knew you well enough to ask a jeweler to open his shop at 4:00 a.m. the morning I left. I don't know what happened to the ring—''

"Josie has it. She wanted to give it to me, but I didn't know if… I didn't know who you…''

"Who I'd bought it for?'' His fingers tightened on her nape. "For you, Sabrina. Only you. How could you think otherwise?''

"Maybe because we never said the words.'' Tears stung her eyes. "Oh, Jack, we laughed and we loved and then I lost you before we ever said the words. You can't imagine how much I regretted that!''

"I'm saying them now. I love you. I think I've loved you since the moment I saw you snoozing like a lazy cat in the sun. I knew for sure when that damned roof fell in on you. I've never been so scared, then or since, even in that black hole.''

It was the moment Sabrina had dreamed about. Cried over. Never thought she'd have. He was saying the words she never thought she'd hear from him, except in her silent, aching heart.

"I love you, too. I suspected it during that damned elevator ride. I couldn't breathe all the way home that night.''

"Neither could I.'' Something that could have been a groan or a laugh rumbled in his chest. "So, when did you know for sure?''

"Maybe when we made love the first time. Or

when I walked into the diner later and saw you juggling platters of pork chops. I just know it was a done deal when you massaged my feet.''

''That did it for you, huh?'' He brought his forehead down until it rested against hers. ''Did I mention at the time that feet aren't my only talent?''

She gave a little hiccup of laughter. ''I seem to recall words to that effect.''

''You don't know how many hours I spent thinking about your feet. And your knees. And your sweet, tight little tush…among other parts.''

''You don't know how many hours I spent thinking about your various parts, too.'' Sighing, she drew back. ''I should have told you that night, Jack! All these months, I've wished that I had told you!''

A smile started in his eyes. ''You didn't have to. I knew how you felt, Sabrina. I never doubted it, not for a minute.''

''I didn't either, at first,'' she said slowly. ''Then Trey told me about Heather, and I began to doubt not only your feelings, but my own.''

The smile in his eyes froze. ''Trey told you about Heather?''

''He came to see me after you…after the explosion. He told me he'd been with you right before you left for Qatar, that you'd talked about me. He said you…you cared for me, far more than you cared about Heather.''

Jack's low, vicious oath shattered the few moments of peace they'd found in each other's touch.

"*Cared* for you? Is that what the bastard said?"

Fury tore through him, ripping apart the calm he'd fought so hard to achieve in the shower.

"He was so sincere, Jack, so anxious to assure me that his very sincerity started me doubting. I couldn't help questioning your true feelings, or my own."

Her green eyes pleaded with him to understand. He understood, all right. He understood exactly what Trey had done. Soon, he swore, he'd know why.

"The doubts were awful enough," Sabrina told him, "but when I called and told him about the baby, he frightened me. Badly."

"How?"

"He said your grandfather would stop at nothing to take my baby."

It was close enough to the truth to terrorize anyone, Jack admitted bitterly. Anyone who'd ever picked up a Tulsa newspaper knew that Joseph Wentworth had steamrollered his way to the top in a brutal, back-breaking industry. Once he'd learned about Sabrina and the baby, he would have put all his considerable energies and financial resources into finding her. It was a miracle that Sabrina could bring herself to trust the old man at all.

He didn't realize his thoughts showed so plainly on his face until she answered them.

"I had to turn to your grandfather at the end, Jack. I didn't have any place else to run. He showed up at the hospital the day Beth was born. At that point, I was ready to give her to him. I would've handed her over right then, signed any legal document he put before me, just to keep her safe.''

"Sabrina..."

"That's why we're here," she concluded in a rush. "That's why I haven't left the grounds since Joseph brought Beth and me here. She's safe here."

For now, Jack thought savagely. He wrapped his hands around her upper arms.

"Listen to me, Sabrina. Ali and I left Qatar in the middle of the night on his private jet. We had to stop twice to refuel, then flew straight into Tulsa. I wanted to break the news of my return from the grave to my grandfather myself. I was afraid the shock might bring on another stroke if it wasn't handled right. I also—"

"You what, Jack?"

He wouldn't lie to her, or try to shield her. Not after all she'd been through.

"I also wanted the home court advantage when word leaked that I was alive."

The knowledge that he'd unwittingly led Trey to Sabrina cut into him like a knife. When he realized how little time they had left, the blade twisted. Urgency added a rough edge to his voice.

"I didn't know you were here. I didn't know about the baby. If I had, I wouldn't have come here. I would've flown into D.C. and baited the trap there."

She paled. "What trap?"

"It took me a while, but I figured out who was behind the attacks on me...and on you. I'm still shaky on why, but I'll know that soon."

"What are you planning?" She curled both hands on his shirt. "Oh, God, you're going to offer yourself as bait, aren't you?"

"I'm going to spring a trap. There's a difference."

Her fingers dug into the wrinkled white cotton. "How long do we have before this trap springs?"

"A few hours. A day at the most. The FAA has probably already notified the State Department that an aircraft belonging to the Royal House of Qatar landed in Tulsa an hour ago. Someone's going to ask who was aboard damned soon, if they haven't already. It won't take long for the information to reach the right desk and the wrong man."

"Trey?" she whispered.

"Trey."

His jaw tight, Jack pried her hands loose and speared a glance at the bassinet.

"Get your things together, yours and Beth's. I'll call up to the big house to let my grandfather know that I'm taking you both out of here."

"To where?"

"To my sister's. Your sister's. Anywhere but here. McGill knows this is where I'll come first."

He spun around, his mind racing and his chest hammering with the need to protect her and his child.

"It won't take more than fifteen minutes to roll out the helo and preflight it. We can decide the safest destination when we're in the air."

Sabrina followed him into the living room and

grabbed his arm. He swung back, impatient, worried, coiled tight and hard.

"I won't run anymore!" she said fiercely. "And I won't let you take that bastard on alone."

"Dammit, this isn't the time for heroics. I need you safe. I need the baby safe. Then I need to focus everything I've got on McGill."

Anger blazed in her eyes, green and searing in its intensity.

"You can't shake it, can you, Jack? Whatever it was that pulled you into your shadowy double life still has you in its thrall. You still think you have to go after the bad guys single-handed, guns blazing, like some damned rogue mercenary."

When this was over, Jack decided, he'd have to explain the fine distinctions of covert operations. Mercenaries got paid for their work. He'd never been in the game for money. Nor was he in it anymore. Sabrina didn't give him the chance to say so, however.

"Now you listen to me, Jack Wentworth. I won't let you go after the bad guys, single-handed or otherwise. If you're serious about us, you're out of the danger business. I lost you once, and I won't lose you again!"

Despite the urgency rippling through his body like small electric currents, Jack had to fight a smile. A few moments ago, she'd suggested that they exercise caution. Take it slow. He didn't read caution in her eyes now. He read anger and determination and a fierce, possessive love that fired his own.

"I'm not going after McGill," he told her. "He'll track me down here, and I'll be waiting for him."

He stilled her protest with a quick, hard kiss.

"I won't be waiting alone. I promise you. Now go gather whatever you need for you and the baby and let's get out of here."

Chapter 15

Edgy and anxious, Jack stood beside Sabrina while she tucked the baby into a plastic carrier with such curves and bends and complicated parts that it looked like something right off the space shuttle. He was so astonished by the amount of materiel and complex logistics involved in transporting one small infant that he almost missed the faint tinkle. It sounded like glass breaking, and it came from the kitchen.

His every sense kicked into overdrive. Instinctively, he filtered out the sounds of Sabrina's soft cooing and the crackling fire in the stone hearth. If he hadn't spent so many months with nothing to do except think and listen to the darkness around him, he might not have picked up the soft, almost inaudible crunch. Cursing himself all over again for flying

straight back to Oklahoma instead of confronting Mc-
Gill in D.C., Jack clapped a hand over Sabrina's
mouth.

"Take the baby and get out the front door," he
whispered in her ear. "Now!"

She threw a single, frightened glance at him over
her shoulder. Whatever she saw in his face stilled any
questions, any argument she might have formed. She
snatched up the plastic carrier and headed for the front
door. The door had swung open to the night when
suddenly she spun around.

"The Beretta!" she whispered in panic. "It's in
my— Oh!"

Her gasp spiraled into a small, choked shriek as the
swinging door from the kitchen crashed inward
against the wall.

If Jack had been alone at that moment, he would
have lunged for the lamp beside the sofa and sent it
smashing to the floor, leaving the living room illuminated only by low, leaping flames. He would have
used the shadows and his familiarity with the guest
house to his advantage. He would have taken down
the bastard who stood frozen in the doorway.

With Sabrina and the baby in the line of fire of
Trey McGill's silenced weapon, he opted instantly for
Plan B. Calmly, deliberately, he took two steps sideways and put himself between them and his former
partner. His only hope was to buy a few, precious
seconds.

The State Department bureaucrat didn't try to disguise the hate that spit from his gray eyes. "I thought I'd taken care of you, Wentworth."

"You tried."

"I didn't know they'd pulled you out of the sea! All these months, I didn't know!"

"Or you would have had them kill me."

"Yes!"

Hate and desperation made McGill's face a haggard mask. If Jack had passed his former partner on the street, he might not have recognized him. Trey had lost weight in the past months. Not as much as Jack, but enough to give his eyes a hollow, haunted look.

"I couldn't believe it when my informant in the consulate called to tell me the prince's private plane had just taken off...with him and a friend aboard."

Jack's mouth twisted. "So, now we know the source of the leaks."

"The knowledge won't do you any good, Wentworth. Damn you, why couldn't you just stay dead!" A muscle ticked in his cheek. The hand that held the gun shook.

That tremor raised the hairs on the back of Jack's neck. He'd suspected McGill had gone over the edge. When Sabrina added her pieces of the puzzle to his a little while ago, he'd been sure. Now, he saw the physical proof.

"Get out of here, Sabrina," he said, keeping his voice flat and calm. "This is between me and McGill."

"No! Don't move! Either of you!"

"I'm the one you want." Jack kept Trey's gaze trained on him. "I'm the one you set up."

Get out, Sabrina. Take the baby and run!

He shouted the order in his mind. Every second, with every breath, he strained to hear a whisper of retreating footsteps. With every ounce of his being, he willed her to use the cover his body provided.

Get out!

"You don't want to hurt her." He held Trey's eyes. "You can't want to hurt an innocent child."

"Innocent!"

The once smooth bureaucrat lost it then. His lips pulled back. His hand shook even more. His words were a snarl, a cry of pain.

"Who are you to talk about innocence, Wentworth? Heather was innocent, and you killed her. She died in my arms."

Jack caught the faint, almost inaudible movement behind him and could have wept with relief. He didn't turn, didn't take his eyes from McGill. He had to give Sabrina time to get away, to get the baby to safety. Without seeming to move a muscle, he edged closer to Trey. He was taller, broader than his one-time partner, even with all the pounds he'd shed. He blocked McGill's view of the room behind his back and spoke faster, louder, to cover Sabrina's escape.

"I couldn't give Heather what she wanted, Trey, and I never promised what I couldn't give."

"No, you couldn't love her! But I did, Wentworth.

I loved her so much I died, too, that night. I swore you'd pay for what you did to her. It took me two years, but I made sure you paid.''

Jack judged the distance between them. He couldn't make it, not with the gun pointed at his chest.

''I thought I'd settled the score when that offshore rig went up in flames,'' Trey raved. ''You killed Heather, and you died for it. Then there was only one more bit of business to take care of. I had to visit your last victim. I had to convince her that you *cared* for her, just as you *cared* for Heather. Destroying her illusions was my last revenge on the late, great Jack Wentworth.'' His face twisted. ''Until the bitch told me she was pregnant.''

He jerked to one side, searching the shadows feathering the far side of the room. Jack moved with him, blocking the view, forcing his attention back to him.

''So, you went after Sabrina?''

''The knowledge that you'd left her pregnant ate at me. I had to kill her, too, before she could spawn another Wentworth. I knew she was here. I was biding my time to get at her. Then you came back from the dead and forced my hand!''

''How did you get onto the grounds, Trey? How did you get past security?''

McGill was soaring now, high on adrenaline and his own cleverness. So high, he didn't notice Jack edge forward an inch, then another.

''Hey, I'm in the same game you were, remember? I didn't spend as many years in field as you did, but

I know how to bypass a damned security system when I have to.''

Jack didn't think so. He'd overseen the installation of the latest modification to this system himself. Alarms had to be flashing in the big house. Someone would be coming to check, would meet Sabrina and the baby on their way across the yard, would shield them.

Time had just about run out for Trey McGill.

He didn't realize it, though. His pale gray eyes now blazed with the blood lust of a predator who'd cornered a wounded prey at last.

"I don't know how you returned from the dead like some damned ghoul, and right now I don't care. This time, I'll make sure you die.''

"McGill…''

"I'm going to shoot the woman first, then the brat. You can watch them both die. I only hope to hell you suffer as much as I suffered before I kill you, too.''

Deliberately, he stepped to the side and swung the gun toward the shadows. Jack knew he wouldn't get another chance. He launched himself through the air.

A pop sounded right beside his ear.

He saw a streak of red fire.

Someone screamed.

Not McGill, he realized in an instant of sheer panic. Oh, God! Not McGill!

Jack crashed into the other man with the echo of that scream knifing into his gut. His fists closed on McGill's wrist. He jerked Trey's arm upward just as the silenced weapon spit another tongue of fire.

Slammed his arm down with everything in him. Heard the crunch of bone against hard, unyielding wood.

Months of deprivation had taken their toll. Before he went to Qatar, Jack could have wrestled the gun out of Trey's hand in two seconds flat and crushed his windpipe with a single, hard-edged chop. Now he gritted his teeth and rolled across the floor, grappling with the flailing, fighting, desperate man.

Suddenly, another shot exploded, deafening him. Jack felt McGill jerk under him. His ears ringing, he tore the gun from the writhing man's grasp. With complete disregard for the red stain blossoming on McGill's left shoulder, he crashed his fist into the bastard's jaw. McGill jerked again, then lay still.

Panting, Jack got one foot under him and pushed himself up.

"Jack!"

She was safe! The message hammered into his brain at the same instant Sabrina dropped the Beretta onto the sofa. Sobbing, shaking, she fell to her knees beside him.

"Are you all right?" Her hands frantic, she patted his chest, his face, his shoulders. "Are you hurt? Were you hit?"

He caught her hands in a hard grip. "I'm okay. What about you? Where's the baby?"

"She's outside," Sabrina panted. "I had to get her out of the line of fire, but I couldn't leave you, Jack.

I couldn't lose you a second time. I couldn't run away again.''

He swallowed twice, forcing down a lethal combination of cold fear and hot anger at the risks she'd taken.

She speared a glance at the unmoving McGill.

''Is he dead?''

''Not unless a shoulder wound and a fist to the chin prove fatal.''

Reluctant relief and fierce disappointment battled on her face for a moment. Relief won out. She was a fighter, Jack acknowledged with silent admiration, but no killer. He pushed to his feet, bringing Sabrina with him.

''Go get the baby. I'll take care of McGill.''

She'd just retrieved the fretting baby and was trying to soothe her when the sound of running footsteps brought her head up with a jerk.

''Oh, God!''

Jack dived for the Beretta. His instincts told him Trey had hunted his prey alone, but he'd gone well beyond taking any chances.

''Cover the baby!''

Sabrina flew across the living room and snatched up the baby's carrier, startling a mewling cry out of the infant. She barely had time to throw herself behind a bend of the wall before the front door burst open.

A small army of men charged through, faces grim, weapons drawn. Five of them Jack identified instantly. His brother, Michael, led the pack. Ali was right behind him. The chief of security for the estate and one of his men came hard on the prince's heels. Jack blinked in surprise at seeing his old buddy, Sam Arquette, barrel in, but didn't have a clue as to the identity of the razor-cheeked Native American or the muscled prizefighter who stood shoulder to shoulder beside Sam.

He intended to find out, though. Particularly since the dark-haired prizefighter went straight to a still-shaking Sabrina and folded her into his arms.

"Jack!"

Michael's exclamation drew Jack's attention from the other two. Uncocking his weapon, Michael slipped it into a holster and rushed across the room. The brothers met in a bear hug and pounded each other joyfully on the back.

"I couldn't believe it when Joseph called us all together and announced that you'd come back," the younger Wentworth said gruffly. His throat worked for a moment. "I *told* him you were too damned stubborn to die!"

Jack grinned. "You were right."

Michael gave his brother a final thump on the back. "I'd just recovered from hearing you'd returned from the dead when the alarms started lighting up the master control panel like a Christmas tree. Everyone at the house just about had a heart attack then."

"Yeah, well, the adrenaline was pumping here, too."

"So I see." Michael's handsome face hardened as he glanced at the figure sprawled on the floor. "If that's the bastard who's been after Sabrina, he'd better not wake up anytime soon or I'll be tempted to take a shot at him, too."

"That's the bastard."

While Ali spit oaths in several different languages, Sam Arquette walked to the unconscious man. His tall frame moved with the same athletic grace Jack remembered from their long-ago navy days.

"What the heck are you doing here, Sam?"

"I came for your daughter's christening tomorrow. We all did."

Hunkering down on one heel, he eyed McGill's oozing shoulder wound.

"He'll live," Sam announced with a definite note of regret. "One of us better get on the radio to the house and tell Amanda we need her."

"Who's Amanda?"

"Sam's wife," Michael supplied as the chief of security's radio cackled.

"Wife!"

It took several seconds for Jack to absorb the welcome news that his friend's grief over the death of his first wife had finally eased enough for him to remarry. While he did, the tough-looking individual with the black eyes and black hair that proclaimed his Native American heritage knelt beside Sam. Rolling the now moaning McGill over, he snapped a pair of cuffs on his wrists with a quick efficiency that said he'd performed that task a few times before.

Leaving McGill in their competent supervision, Jack turned his attention to the man comforting Sabrina and the still fretful baby. Crossing to where they stood, he held out his hand.

"I don't know who you are, but thanks for coming to the rescue."

His handshake was returned with a strong, sure grip. "You didn't need much rescuing, but you're welcome. The name's Carter, Max Carter." A smile softened his tanned, rugged features. "I'm Sabrina's cousin...and your brother-in-law."

"You want to run that one by me one more time?" Jack said slowly.

"Josie's married," Michael interjected, joining the small group. A lopsided grin tugged at his mouth. "Me, too," he added.

The oldest of the Wentworth siblings was still reeling from that bit of news when Sabrina looped an arm around the trim, dark-eyed man who'd wielded the handcuffs with such expertise.

"And this is my brother-in-law, Riley Hunter." Her eyes lit with laughter as she expanded on the introduction. "He arrested my twin, thinking Rachel was me, before she—"

"He didn't arrest me."

Everyone turned as a brunette with Sabrina's striking features and deep green eyes strode through the open front door.

"He only threatened to."

She was followed in quick order by a brown-haired woman with a medical bag, a petite blond with startlingly turquoise eyes and Josie. Crying, laughing, sobbing out his name, Josie threw herself into Jack's arms...at which point he discovered his sister was not only married, but pregnant.

His grandfather's arrival with a man Jack learned was Sabrina's father and a long, loud wail from the baby turned the scene into one of utter chaos and joyous confusion. In the midst of it all, Josie slipped a small velvet jeweler's box into Jack's hand.

"This was in with your...your..." she gulped, blinking back a rush of tears "...your personal effects. I tried to give it to Sabrina when we found her and the baby, but she didn't want to... She wasn't sure..."

Jack's gaze sliced through the noise and confusion to the woman whose image he'd held in his heart for so many months. The expression in her eyes as she met his told him that she was sure now. As sure as he was.

"Thanks, Josie," he said with a smile for Sabrina alone. "I'll take it from here."

Epilogue

It was, according to the *Tulsa World News,* the social event of the year. What had been planned as a christening, to be attended by only the closest family and friends of the wealthy, influential Wentworth clan, metamorphosed overnight into a christening *and* a wedding. Both, the society reporter assured her readers, would be talked about for decades to come.

The christening dampened every eye in the church.

The wedding produced a veritable flood of joyous tears.

An exquisite, four-carat emerald-cut diamond sparkled on the bride's ring finger. She wore white satin and rivers of priceless white lace. The same veil, the reporter hastened to point out, had been worn by Jack Wentworth's mother at her wedding.

Ms. Sabrina Jensen was given in marriage by her father, Mr. Frank Jensen, and attended by her sister, Mrs. Riley Hunter, of Oklahoma City, and her sisters-in-law, Mrs. Max Carter and Mrs. Michael Wentworth. The Misses Caroline and Sara Arquette, daughters of Mr. and Mrs. Sam Arquette, served as flower girls.

The groomsmen included Mr. Michael Wentworth, Mr. Sam Arquette, and Prince Ali Fashor Kaisal, of the Royal House of Qatar.

A reception followed the wedding and christening ceremonies, catered by a Mr. Hank Donovan of the Route 66 Diner. More than five hundred guests feasted on succulent chicken-fried steak smothered in sizzling onions, Oklahoma home fries, and burn-your-mouth stewed okra.

After a nostalgic and oh-so romantic honeymoon spent driving the old Route 66 from Chicago to California, Mr. and Mrs. Wentworth intend to take up residence in Tulsa, where he'll continue to direct the far-flung Wentworth Oil Works conglomerate and she'll oversee operations of the diner she recently purchased and enthusiastically predicts will be the first of many.

When the groom toasted his bride, it was no exaggeration to say that there wasn't a dry eye among the many happy guests. He spoke of a love that transcended loss, fear, even death. A love, he said with a smile that made even this somewhat jaded reporter's heart skip several beats, that would last forever.

* * * * *

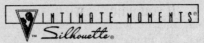

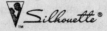

If you enjoyed what you just read,
then we've got an offer you can't resist!

Take 2 bestselling
love stories FREE!
Plus get a FREE surprise gift!

Clip this page and mail it to Silhouette Reader Service™

IN U.S.A.	**IN CANADA**
3010 Walden Ave.	P.O. Box 609
P.O. Box 1867	Fort Erie, Ontario
Buffalo, N.Y. 14240-1867	L2A 5X3

YES! Please send me 2 free Silhouette Intimate Moments® novels and my free surprise gift. Then send me 6 brand-new novels every month, which I will receive months before they're available in stores. In the U.S.A., bill me at the bargain price of $3.57 plus 25¢ delivery per book and applicable sales tax, if any*. In Canada, bill me at the bargain price of $3.96 plus 25¢ delivery per book and applicable taxes**. That's the complete price and a savings of over 10% off the cover prices—what a great deal! I understand that accepting the 2 free books and gift places me under no obligation ever to buy any books. I can always return a shipment and cancel at any time. Even if I never buy another book from Silhouette, the 2 free books and gift are mine to keep forever. So why not take us up on our invitation. You'll be glad you did!

245 SEN CNFF
345 SEN CNFG

Name	(PLEASE PRINT)	
Address	Apt.#	
City	State/Prov.	Zip/Postal Code

* Terms and prices subject to change without notice. Sales tax applicable in N.Y.
** Canadian residents will be charged applicable provincial taxes and GST.
   All orders subject to approval. Offer limited to one per household.
   ® are registered trademarks of Harlequin Enterprises Limited.

INMOM99   ©1998 Harlequin Enterprises Limited

This March Silhouette is proud to present

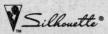

SENSATIONAL

MAGGIE SHAYNE
BARBARA BOSWELL
SUSAN MALLERY
MARIE FERRARELLA

This is a special collection of four complete novels for one low price, featuring a novel from each line: Silhouette Intimate Moments, Silhouette Desire, Silhouette Special Edition and Silhouette Romance.

Available at your favorite retail outlet.

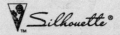

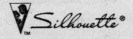

FORTUNE'S *Children*™

*The Fortune family requests
the honor of your presence at the weddings of*

FORTUNE'S CHILDREN™

The Brides

Silhouette Desire's scintillating new miniseries,
featuring the beloved Fortune family
and five of your favorite authors.

The Honor Bound Groom—**January 1999**
by Jennifer Greene (SD #1190)

Society Bride—**February 1999**
by Elizabeth Bevarly (SD #1196)

And look for more **FORTUNE'S CHILDREN:
THE BRIDES** installments by Leanne Banks,
Susan Crosby and Merline Lovelace,
coming in spring 1999.

Available at your favorite retail outlet.

Silhouette®

Look us up on-line at: http://www.romance.net   SDFORTUNE

INTIMATE MOMENTS®
Silhouette®

COMING NEXT MONTH

#913 ROYAL'S CHILD—Sharon Sala
The Justice Way

Royal Justice knew he would do anything to make his daughter happy. So when she insisted that a lone hitchhiker needed *their* help, he went against his better judgment and told Angel Rojas to climb on board. After that, it didn't take long before his two favorite females were giving him a few lessons on how to live—and love—again.

#914 CULLEN'S BRIDE—Fiona Brand
March Madness

Sexy Cullen Logan thought he had no chance for a happy family—until he met Rachel Sinclair. She was everything he'd ever wanted in a woman, and now she was about to have his child. Cullen knew that being a father was a full-time job, but given his dangerous past, was he qualified for the position?

#915 A TRUE-BLUE TEXAS TWOSOME—Kim McKade
March Madness

Toby Haskell was perfectly content with his life as a country sheriff. Until his one true love, Corrine Maxwell, returned to town. Losing her had been hard—and accepting it even harder. Now she was back, and he knew he had a second chance. But was his small-town life enough for a big-city girl?

#916 THE MAN BEHIND THE BADGE—Vickie Taylor
March Madness

The last thing FBI agent Jason Stateler needed was to get too close to his sexy female partner. But Lane McCullough was part of the case, and he knew she wasn't going away—and, secretly, he didn't really want her to. Tracking down a criminal was easy—it was their unexpected passion that was going to be the problem.

#917 DANGEROUS CURVES—Kristina Wright
March Madness

Samantha Martin knew she was innocent of murder—she'd just been in the wrong place at the wrong time. And so was Jake Cavanaugh, because he had been foolish enough to pick her up when she was making her escape. But now there was no turning back, and before long she was trusting him with her life…but what about with her heart?

#918 THE MOTHER OF HIS CHILD—Laurey Bright
Conveniently Wed

The moment Charisse Lane most feared had arrived: her child's father had found them! More disconcerting was her immediate, intense attraction to the tall, dark dad—an attraction Daniel Richmond clearly reciprocated. But Charisse knew that a legacy of lies—and secrets—could very well prevent the happily-ever-after she wished could be theirs....